THROUGH TH 'TAR

C000196262

DrkFetyshNyghts

THROUGH THE EYES OF 'TARA'

FETISH WORLD BOOKS

A FETISH WORLD BOOKS PAPERBACK

© Copyright 2017
DrkFetyshNyghts

The right of DrkFetyshNyghts to be identified as author
of this work has been asserted in accordance with the
Copyright, Designs and Patents Act 1988.

All Rights Reserved.

No reproduction, copy or transmission of the publication
may be made without written permission. No paragraph
of this publication may be reproduced, copied or
transmitted save with the written permission of the
publisher, or in accordance with the provisions of the
Copyright Act 1956 (as amended).

Any person who does any unauthorised act in relation to
this publication may be liable to criminal prosecution
and civil claims for damages.

ISBN: 978 1 78695 109 0

FETISH WORLD BOOKS
is an imprint of
Fiction4All

Published 2017
Fiction4All

Chapter 1

The Early Years

I don't know what mum was thinking when she called me Tara! I mean what WAS she thinking? I'd like to be able to blame dad, but I haven't got a dad. And mum didn't ever want to talk about him no matter which way I tried to bring it up. Some of my friends were surprised I'm not upset by not having a dad. I guess I could be but then it's not like he was there and then all of a sudden he went and didn't come back. I've never had a dad. At least I can't remember a dad ever being round. So, it's a case of not missing what you never had. It's always been just me and mum. Me and mum against the world! Fuck the world!

At least that was what it was like, before. Before the night out. I try to think of that night as something other than 'a night out'. But that was what it was. I don't want to dwell on that now though. That night changed things forever. It changed things that could never be unchanged. But I don't want to think about that now either. I need a rest from that. I need to rest my mind from that. There's too much in there. Too much in my mind. It's like I have to take a step back and at least try to block it all out. I can't of course. Blocking it out is never an option. All I can do is think about the old days. Days with mum. The fun we used to have. You know, we were more like sisters than mum and daughter. We used to do everything together. My friends couldn't believe we were so close. But the fact was that we were. We were as close as it was possible to get. Mum was 'fun'. She taught me how to do my hair. How to do my makeup. How to dress. She even taught me how to dress and makeup if I was ever 'out on the pull'. How's that for a cool mum? We used to laugh so much about that. Everyone thought mum was so cool. And she was.

Yeah, yeah, I know that sounds bad but it wasn't a bad thing. It was all only ever a light-hearted thing. We used to do it for a laugh. She would overdo the makeup on me and then I would do it on her. Then she would choose a dress, or skirt and top combination for me that was 'way' over the top for a girl my age, and then I would do the same with her. Except with her it would be a selection that was far to 'young' for her. Then we would roll about in fits of laughter. Giggling like little schoolgirls at the 'look' we had achieved for each other.

I loved my mum so much. That's what hurts now for split seconds at a time, if I can see past the orgasmic state that I'm addicted to. That's why even as I write this, the tears are running down my face. My mascara is a mess already and its only 8am. Yes, mascara at 8am. It's what I'm used to now. It's what I do. It's what I have to do now. I have a set of rules and regulations that I have to live by and I cannot swerve away from these rules and regulations. It's what I have to do. Those rules and regulations are basically my life. Those and, and the addictions. Well, the addiction, there is only one addiction and believe me when I say that that is enough.

I used to watch my mum - ever since I was very young. There was a girl down the road. Well to me she wasn't a girl, she was a woman, and she would come and sit with me when mum went out. She always went out at nights. Mostly at weekends - like the Thursday, Friday and Saturday night - always those nights but sometimes other nights as well. And she would always be dressed and made up to the nines. By always done up to the nines I mean she would always have a lot of makeup on. And her skirts were always short. I always remember thinking that mum had the best legs. She always had the best legs and the highest heels. It was a fact as well that mum had the best breasts. It was weird how I used to watch her like this. She would go out early in the night and I would always be fast asleep when she returned. Very rarely would I hear her coming in. Most of the time I had no idea what time she came in. And yet every morning when I woke up, there she was bright and breezy. Refreshed and ready for a new day. And more often than not she would get me something, buy me something nice. Mum was good like that. The best.

One time she came in at some unearthly hour, and I was awake. My bedroom door creaked open but I pretended to be asleep. Mum came and sat on the bed. I don't know why I pretended to be asleep, maybe because it was real late and I didn't want her to think I was losing out on sleep, I don't know. But she used her fingers and was brushing my hair off my face. And then she leant down and kissed me and whispered, "I love you baby girl." I wasn't exactly a baby girl but I was very, very young. And as she did that her warm breath washed over me. There was the smell of cigarettes and alcohol. I didn't know it was that then, but looking back I know it now. Then she left. I kept my eyes closed and was smiling to myself. Mum always made me feel good even though I didn't really know where she went to at night. I sensed her pausing at the bedroom door and looking at me before she silently backed out and clicked the door shut. I don't know what it was but I always, always felt safe with mum around. It was like she wasn't fazed. Like she wasn't worried by anything that life could throw at her or us.

I don't care where she went to at night. One girl who wasn't my friend once told me that her mum had told her that my mum was a prostitute. She had announced it like it was supposed to knock me for six or something. The fact was that it didn't knock me for six. I just shrugged, not that I even really knew what a prostitute was back then, and laughed at her. She was more hurt than me. Now I think mum was doing what she had to do. She was a single mother raising a daughter and making her money the way she knew how. That didn't make her a bad woman, or a bad mother. It made her exactly the opposite in my eyes. I never thought bad of my mother for what she did to make money. I never thought bad of her at all. Ever! I did think though that the way she was, what she had to do, did shape our relationship and what we did for fun. The dressing up, the making up. It was innocent, just innocent fun. Mum using her skills the way she knew how to amuse and be close to her little girl. I could never hold that against her. Some might cringe at the upbringing and childhood I had, but I don't. I had a mother who loved me more than some collective mums and dads love their spoilt, have-everything kids so I didn't care.

I often wish it was back in the day now. If only I could get those days back. But I can't and I know that I can't. Those days will never come back. Too much water has passed under the bridge. Too much has happened to me. I don't even know where mum is now. They told me she had moved away and forgotten about me. I don't believe that but at the same time I do believe it. They did things to her. Told her that she would be an addict as well. Who 'they' are cannot be disclosed as I write this - maybe later though when I can think more straight. Rather who they are will become evident in time. As I write I am expecting any time to hear the approach of high heels outside the locked door. It will be as much as I can do when I hear those high heels, not to pee myself. I have to try not to. It's not good if I pee myself. But then it's not good to hear those heels either. Because when I hear them I know that something is going to happen again. I'll just spend this time thinking and

8

remembering the times with my mum. That's like a place I can escape to. It's getting harder to escape like that. Much, much harder.

Like the time when she held a party for my tenth birthday - I think it was my tenth birthday - yes, I'm sure it was. I never had that many friends. My mum was always my bestest friend. So, mum just invited the whole year in my school. She hired the town hall and there were all these tables laid out with what seemed to be loads and loads of food. I said to her, "mum we're never gonna eat all this." It just seemed like loads and loads of food and this was before anyone at all had turned up. I stood at one end of the hall and there were just rows of tables with all this food on. Sandwiches, bits of sausage on sticks. Cheese and pineapple on sticks. Cake, jelly, spoons ready for ice cream. It really was the whole works and at the time it seemed that everything was 'big'. That everything was over the top. I realise now that it wasn't all that spectacular, or all that big. It just seemed that way. Mum told me, "You wait and see. There will be loads and loads here, you'll see." And with that she did one of those cheeky little winks she used to give me.

I used to crack up at that wink. It was cheeky and yet it was kind of sexy as well. I didn't know what sexy was back then. But when I think now, yeah that's what it was. It was as though mum had this insight or some kind of crystal ball into how this day would be. And she was right you know! When the time came and no-one had come I had thought no-one was going to turn up to my party and that it would be just be me and mum. I remember thinking that I didn't really care. As long as mum was there we could have a good time. We did have a good time. And then, just past the time, girls and boys started to turn up and be dropped off by their parents. It was like it was just a minute or so past the time that the party was supposed to start, but it seemed longer. It

9

seemed much, much longer. It was like no-one wanted to be the first to arrive. Or no-one wanted to arrive before the time stipulated on the invites.

Then all these people, all these boys and girls just came and they all bought me cards and presents. I had never had a birthday party before. Mum was always out on my birthday. She would always come home and slip money into my card for me because she had never had time to go shopping for a present. But I was kind of alright with that. I kind of liked the money better. Of course, back then, I didn't really know where the money came from. It didn't matter anyway. But this evening she didn't go out. It was like she had made a stand and decided that she wouldn't go wherever she usually went to at nights. She would stay with me because I had reached some milestone - my tenth birthday, double figures, and it was a Friday. I remembered that always. No wonder really when you find out what happened.

It was weird really, I was convinced that no-one really liked me at school and that if anything, most of the kids my age gave me a wide birth. I never knew why I thought or felt like this it was just something that was there in my mind. And yet here they all were coming to my party. And not just coming to my party because it was a free feed, but coming to my party bringing me cards and presents. I felt like a princess. Yes, that is what I felt like back then on that evening. I felt like a true princess. If I think about it now, that was the best night of my life. It was like I was the centre of attention. I had all these kids crowded around me wanting to be my friend and being nice to me. I can't think of one, not one single kid, boy or girl who was there that night that was horrible to me. It was like I was in some kind of twilight zone. Or maybe it was just a case that I had been imagining the other kids not liking me before I don't know.

Everything was perfect that night. Everything that is except the clown. I have no idea where the clown came from or who he or she was. Mum had arranged it. Once the food was all but gone and everyone was just chilling the clown came. It would be true to say that no-one knew whether this clown was male or female. That was mostly because the way he or she was made up and dressed was literally so 'scary' that it didn't matter if it was male or female. There had been this anticipation before the clown came on. No-one had caught sight of it before it actually appeared in front of all the chairs, so there was this anticipation in the air. Like an expectation and an excitement. And then when it did finally come on, there was just this silence. Utter silence and nothing else. It didn't so much walk out in front of us all as stumble or peg leg it out. And it wasn't a happy clown, or a clumsy clown, or one with a funny walk. It was just out and out scary.

For a start there was the thick downturned mouth. Not a happy smiley face. That was painted on thickly as you would expect but it was painted on in a fashion that looked more like a grimace. A downturned sad grimace but also with a hint of sharp pointy teeth. There was just this collective sucking in of air as this 'thing' came out and just stood there. And that was the thing it just stood there. I feel guilty about saying 'it' but even now all these years later and with what I have been through, and am going through, that clown was an 'it' and an 'it' not in a good way. But it did, it just stood there. It didn't say anything and it didn't mime anything. There was no funny walk, or falling over. There were no tumbles, or trips, or magic tricks. There was just this monster of a clown that just stood there. And it seemed to look at every single one of us kids. It seemed to do that one at a time and then hold that gaze. It was as though it caught the eyes of the individual and then just held that stare in a scary way. I can't describe the 'silence' that descended in that place when this was going on. It was just like a thick silence. Yes that's it, a thick silence.

I remember flicking my eyes to my mum and she looked mortified. That told me that this clown, this monster clown was not what she had expected or ordered for a kid's party. It was like one at a time it sucked the life out of the particular kid it was staring at. And the oddest thing was that everyone was like stuck to the spot. No-one moved away from this clown. No-one tried to get out of the grasp of its stare. This is how I remembered it. This monster clown in a big loose baggy suit but with that scary face. The downturned mouth that would depict sadness. The hint at pointy teeth that depicted a monster. And then the eyes. The eyes were more horrific than anything and that were finished off with tears of blood dripping from underneath. I can say now, what was that person thinking? What on earth would this person be thinking to turn up at a kid's party and do this 'act'. Even if there had been a mistake and this person thought he was going to an adult party, or some kind of horror event, then he or she had time to turn it around when they actually turned up. Once they realised that it was a kid's party they could have either changed the act or left.

But that wasn't the way it happened. That wasn't how it panned out. And there it was. Just standing there, staring at each and every one of the kids one at a time. Just standing there with its arms limp at its sides. Staring and seeming to suck the life out of each and every kid. That was what I could never understand - why me, or any of the other kids, or why mum didn't kind of break the spell and then get rid of the monster clown. I don't know. It was like what would happen if the spell was broken?

It had been just a brilliant day and evening - one that couldn't have gone any better. And then there was this at the end of it. And that standing staring, monster clown might have only been there a few minutes. Not even a few minutes but it seemed longer. It seemed like it was there doing that staring thing for ages and ages. And then, when it was all quiet, when it was a fact that this person, he or she, had the full attention of everyone in that town hall, it seemed to let out a single, nerve tingling grunt before turning and walking off. It walked off out of sight and was not seen again. At least it wouldn't be seen by me for a long, long time.

And once it had done that - once that monster clown had plodded off, the same way that it had plodded on there was just this silence left. Like an awe inspired silence. Or more like a shocked silence. The kids, my friends didn't have a thing to say not even amongst themselves. My mum was just standing there. She had followed this thing every step of its way with her eyes. And she had gone pale herself. I'd never seen my mum like that before. Nothing ever phased mum and she was and we were so, so close. But this thing had spooked her. That much was clear - that she had been spooked by this clown. Everyone there that night had been spooked. Spooked or scared stiff.

I was the first to move. I moved to my mum and held her hand. Her hand felt cold and clammy. I think now I look back, this clown had scared her or something. "Where did you find that mum?" It was all I could think of to ask and by this time all the others were starting to move as well. The spell had finally been broken and people were coming round. My mum didn't answer me when I asked her that. She never would say or even mention that clown again. The party was often referred to, but never the clown. It was like that fucked up clown was a forbidden subject.

13

That was odd. I didn't think about it at the time. The clown was horrific but it hadn't disturbed me. I didn't have a party as such again. From that year I began to grow up. From that party I got friends, real friends and I began to spread my wings. And the thing was that mum never stopped or tried to halt that spreading of my wings. It was like she was letting me grow up. It was like she was letting me mature and blossom into a young woman. She was always there for me. She was always there on hand with words of wisdom and words of advice but she never overdid it, except maybe with makeup and party dress advice. She only ever really stood back and watched her little girl, her little princess grow up. And that was the thing, I did grow up.

Chapter 2

7 years later

We were like the red lip brigade. Me and mum. It didn't matter how hard I tried, I couldn't get my lips to look like mum could make them look. She would do hers and then she would do mine. As though she was practicing on herself and then perfecting it with mine. I loved it when she did my lips. "You've gotta make 'em want you." That was what she would say to me in that south-eastern accent that was somehow obvious. She had this husky quality to her voice as well. I knew that it was the cigarettes. But I don't know, it was husky and it was 'sexy'. I shouldn't say that about my mum but it was true. Just like that wink was sexy back in the day. I kind of wished that my voice was like hers. I told her that once and she just laughed. "It'll come, you'll see." There was no reason in existence why I wanted that husky cigarette stained voice, other than I just did!

And then there was this night. She was going to town on me. She knew I was making a rare trip into town with friends and she was doing what she did best. She was tarting me up. Something she had always done herself in her younger days. But, my god, mum still looked good - even I knew that. And even I knew that she would never have any trouble pulling a guy. Come to think of it she would never have any trouble pulling another woman. Not that she was that way inclined, that I knew about. That's just my deeper thoughts. "Do I really want them to want me though mum? That is the question." Mum just sipped another drop of her wine and she smiled. And she did that thing where she tilted her head and looked at me all dreamy. "Maybe not now. But you will. No harm in getting in the practice now is there?" I couldn't see anything wrong with that

15

reasoning. It made perfect sense to me. I just giggled and took a gulp of wine myself. Yeah, I know, I was a little under age, but so what. At least I wasn't doing drugs.

It was always an event when I went out. It was like an excuse for mum to get out her makeup kit and 'transform' me into someone else. I didn't mind if I'm honest. It was like a chance to escape the mundane of ordinary normal life. In a way, I think mum was swapping her for me. Her days of going out, those sleazy days had long gone. She had just quit one day. I don't know why. She never said why. It was just like something that she decided on the spur of the moment. She decided she had had enough of that life and just quit. Just like some people quit smoking one day, or drinking. But then it was like she struggled to replace that life with something else. I got it, I really did and for that reason I didn't mind stepping in as that substitute. I didn't mind her transforming me into that someone else. I don't know why, or what the reasoning behind it was, it just excited me. I always, always got excited to know what, or who mum would make me look like next.

And she did go to town on me this time. "That bust of yours, it's just about popping honey. Now you just have to emphasise that a little bit. Just a little bit. Those boobs, those legs and those lips, you're gonna make guys want you big time baby." I always laughed because she got more excited than me. She'd gone to my closets and just taken out a load of things that she would try on me. Change some things, swap some things around and then get the accessories out and chop and change those. The very first thing that she had decided was to go with pantyhose. The reason for that was that the dress, like a tight lycra clubbing dress thing was too short - way too short to wear stockings. And mum deep down was a decent human being. Whatever in life she had had to do to get by, that was one thing, but deep down she was a

16

decent woman. A decent human being. So, going bare legged wasn't her bag at all. I think she saw the sheer nylon crotch of the panty hose as a filter, or as a protection to unwanted attention. And panties over the pantyhose. "You have to be ready when the little girl's room calls baby. Don't wanna be messing with panties under pantyhose hey?"

And we'd giggle about that. "Are you sure about this mum, I mean I look a bit - a bit 'out there' don't you think?" And mum looked me up and down, she tilted her head this way and then that way as though she was considering what I had said. And then she just said her own thing, "You look amazing darling and you just need to carry yourself like you feel amazing. You'll see. It will have the desired result, I promise you." I wasn't sure what the desired result was for mum. I had the feeling that sometimes she was trying to marry me off or something. Like one of those fucked up arranged marriages they do in in third world countries. But it was all light hearted. And you know, I trusted my mum when she dressed and made me up like this. It was a good thing. It made me feel good. And even if I had to admit it to her, it made me feel amazing.

The dress was one shoulder off, one shoulder on and it was almost backless. It was such a delicate, thin dress that it was complex to get on. Thank god mum was there to help me. Definitely, definitely a two-woman job. And it clung to me like a second skin. It was just as well I was getting more and more confident with how I looked. I always remember looking at mum when she was dressed up ready to go out when I was really young and thinking how amazing she looked. And it was from that that I got that I must have looked the same. That I got it from mum. I don't think I ever suffered from some of the stuff teenagers suffered from with body image and all of that. I guess I am just lucky that way. There was hardly any back to the dress so there was plenty of flesh on display. Thank the lord for fake tan! And the front of the dress, although thin and clingy, did what it had to do in pushing my breasts together and squeezing them up a little bit. I'd always wanted breasts like mum. Now her's were 'breasts', proper ones. I kind of saw me with breasts like those one day. And judging by how I was beginning to 'pop' in her words, that day was getting closer and closer.

"These heels mum. They're way too high. I mean like I'm tottering!" And that was the truth. I was tottering. Heels like these were something else that I remembered from mum's past. The spiky heels. No ankle straps to spoil the line of the legs, just court shoes - patent leather and with those lethal metal tipped heels. She had bought me these specially for this night out. I don't know where she got them because they don't do shoes like these on the high street. Mail order perhaps, or on the net. Yes, that would be it. She was always on the net - surfing and shopping, shopping and more shopping. I liked the shoes. They were stupendous to look at. But they took some getting used to, to wear. "Baby, you crack those shoes and you're a made woman for life. Men and boys love heels and what they do to a girl. What they do to a girl's body and her mind." I got what she was saying about what those heels did to the body. They tightened everything up. They forced a strut as opposed to a walk. And they forced the ass to sway and the breasts to kind of roll. I didn't know what she meant by what heels like this did to the mind though. That was just mum being deep I guess. Maybe a little bit over my head. Although with these heels especially I was aware of being tighter than normal and of the little tugs between the legs at my muscles down there. That was kind of weird, but nice as well. My sexual awakening as it were. I knew about sex, and about being wet down there. The first time I had felt myself wet down there I had been scared shitless. I thought I was going to die or something. I thought I was about to bleed out! It was just me growing up - becoming 'me'.

That was it, my sexual awakening. I'd been aware of 'myself' down there for some time. The little sensations that made me gulp sometimes, but kept to myself. So, I guess I knew in the back of my mind what those heels did to my mind meant after all. I just smiled at her and she smiled back. She seemed pleased that I understood what she was talking about. She seemed pleased that I was in that frame of mind. "Tell you what mum, if I am going to 'crack' these heels, one more glass of wine before the taxi gets here - what say you?" And I giggled at her. I was JUST under the legal drinking age. But what the hell. I'd been having a glass of wine with dinner, and a few more besides for the last few years. I didn't abuse alcohol. I was always one of those girls who knew when she had had enough. I had decided long ago that I would make a hopeless alcoholic because my hangovers, if I did overdo it even slightly, were very bad. "Sounds like a plan to me. Tell you what, I'll play mummy." And we cracked up about that. Mummy playing mummy!

I didn't even know mum knew I smoked cigarettes. I didn't do it a lot, just sometimes. Never when I was alone, and never in the house. I was just a social smoker really. Something that made me feel like I was one of the girls. But she offered me a cigarette like she had known forever. I just looked at her. I didn't move my hand to accept the cigarette from the pack. "It's ok honey I know. You can't kid a kidder - remember that. Its ok, just take one." And I did. That threw me a little if I'm honest. It had come out of the blue. But then maybe that was the way that mum thought it would be best handled. And she was right. No big dramas, no big lecture. Just her letting me know that she knew. It hit me then, two sets of deep red lips with cigarettes dangling. That shouldn't have been a good image or a good vision but it was. It didn't just strike me as a good look - mum and daughter together drinking wine, smoking. It should have been the epitome of a very less than savoury scenario. But you know, I didn't care. I didn't care one bit. I felt good. I held mum's hands as she flicked the lighter and held it for me to light my cigarette. I dragged and inhaled, then exhaled and mum watched. I think she was waiting to see if I would cough or not. I didn't of course.

It would have been a contradiction. She had known that I had been smoking for some time so for me to cough now would be odd to say the least. I did dwell how she knew. But not for long. She washed my clothes - she would have smelled cigarette smoke on them. Yes, maybe that was friends I was close to, but this would have been stronger. It would have been obvious that I was smoking myself. It was weird how she watched me. Like she was watching for the smoke to pour from between my red lips. Yeah, that bit of the evening was weird if I am completely honest. There was like this gratification in mum's face - in her smile. As though she had just seen her little one come of age or something. And that was the thing, she did smile. Maybe I'm wrong, but it felt like she was proud of me or something. This will read like some kind of fucked up world - a mum proud of her tarted up little girl, slightly under aged, smoking and drinking before she goes out on the town to make men want her because of the way she looks and all that. How fucked up is that?

That was mum being mum. The thing was that I felt I was my own girl, my own young woman. Yeah it was a little bit weird but hey, I was young. I had the big wide world to explore. I wasn't thinking too much about the height of my heels or what they made me walk or strut like. I wasn't thinking too much about the fact that my lips were too red - or that them being too red might give out the wrong signals. I was just busy having a good time. And mum, she was the only mum I had. The way she was with me was the only way I knew. We weren't ripped apart by what she used to do to make ends meet. Rather we were closer together. We were bonded deeper because of all that. And it would take more than a lycra micro mini dress and heels to rip us apart. That's a fact. We spent another twenty minutes just drinking the wine, smoking and chatting. Then there was the beep of the taxi horn. Time for me to go.

"You and mum been playing dress up again?" That was Candice - she knew the score and it could have been really nastily that she said that, but she didn't. She said it with a smile on her face, just like she always did. I think she was a little bit jealous if I'm honest. Like jealous in the sense that she didn't have a mum like mine, a cool mum. There was this little pub just around the corner from the club that we always went to. We always met up there. They did some really off the wall cocktails. I always made my friends laugh because I sucked cocktail through straw in a way not to mess up my lipstick. Candice would just look and not say anything - I knew what she thought. She thought I looked snobby or something. It was Frankie who'd throw her head back and giggle, "What is going on with that suck Tara?" And that would be that the whole group would crack up. There was Leeza, and Christie, and Brianna and of course Frankie and Candice. Everyone got tarted up in their own way and everyone had their own look going on. We didn't want to look like a colour coordinated girl band on a night out now did we? "Why don't we finish up these drinks and go to the club a bit earlier? We'll get a good table for a change - right next to the dance floor

21

and not too far from the bar." I wasn't quite sure why the not too far from the bar bit got a snigger or two. Or maybe I was. "Yeah sounds like a plan." Leeza spoke and everyone nodded. A unanimous decision!

It was only 10pm and yet the club was bouncing already. There was the usual queue at the door but we bypassed that as members and regulars. It felt kind of good walking the length the queue and all these people who would be there for hours and might not get in at all, just looking. Looking and wondering if we were VIP's or celebrities or something. The usual clique really. New faces in the queue and ones that I knew. I nodded and smiled. I felt more than a few sets of eyes on me. I was used to the heels by this point and my walk was a purposeful strut. I had heard the term slut-strut and that kind of made me smile. I didn't care about that. It was my age - I didn't care about the word 'slut'. It made me laugh. As far as I could tell, men and boys used it all the time. But that was just it, they were men and boys. And when I heard other girls saying it, it was usually because they were jealous of someone they consequentially called a slut. If 'slut' made me feel this good then, sure, give me the label, give me the name I could handle that. Sometimes it was like the way I had been brought up had paid dividends. Like I had been brought up hard in a way and that the bringing up that I had received with my mum prepared me for the big bad world. I was sure that was it.

"You look amazing, let me just tell you that." Right at the head of the queue I had been touched on the arm. I am very sensitive like that, to touch and proximity. I don't know why. Maybe just a couple of my senses in hyper mode. It was a woman, a stunning looking older woman who had touched me. And as she had done that she had slightly stroked my bare arm with her nail. I just smiled. "Thank you so much." And there was this split second in which our eyes met and locked. I cannot even describe it, not really. I'm not sure if it was a connection or what. The woman was older than us. She was more my mum's age, maybe a bit younger, it was hard to tell. But I remember thinking that it was strange to see older people at this place. She was with a big tall, immaculately suited man. He didn't say anything. It was like he hadn't even seen the exchange between the woman and me. He was busy watching what was going on around them. And with that the woman took her hand back and she smiled again. There was something about her smile. She was an attractive woman with a stunning smile - and perfect white teeth. Yes, perfect white teeth. And then we were being ushered into the club by the doormen. I was thinking maybe it was just one of those 'ships that pass in the night' kind of moments that I had just had. Whatever!

I loved this place. It was all underground and with low cave like ceilings. It gave it like a claustrophobic feel, but with a state of the art sound system and hidden base units, the place rocked it really did. In another half an hour there would be no tables to choose from and I spotted the one we wanted before anyone else. Right in front, centre stage - or centre dance floor. We never, but never got that table but we did tonight. I grabbed the table whilst the others went to the bar. This time of night it was just gentle old school R&B coming through the sound system. And that was the thing, the sound seemed to 'fill' that place, literally. No Diggity, Brown Sugar and Gangsta's Paradise, yesssss!

Because I got the table I got the best seat as well. I watched the others at the bar and considered the seats. I looked at them from all angles and then chose one. I reckoned that I would be able to see everything from that seat. And to the corner of my eye there was that couple again - the older couple. They sat just a few tables away

23

and I was aware of the man this time looking my way. I just turned my eyes to him and smiled. He smiled back. A huge handsome man. But then the woman was very attractive as well. She caught my eyes and smiled and lifted her hand in a little wave. At this point I wasn't feeling anything other than I would be having a good night. That was what it was going to be, a good night. At this precise point I didn't have a clue how this night would change. How it would change everything.

Chapter 3

Slowly the volume in the club was getting louder. That never ceased to amaze me - the way they did that. From the smooth classics and then louder and louder and louder. Old school R&B gave way to slightly harder, edgier Hip Hop and house from the 90s and the noughties. I love the way this place ramped it up a little at a time. Coming through the ages with the music. It was funny, I shouldn't have even known most of the earlier stuff but I did. Memories from my childhood. It was from when mum used to go out. She'd have a stereo blasting the tunes. She used to play all the old Motown stuff - she could really groove to Diana Ross and the Supremes, Marvin Gaye and The Four Tops. They were like relics from her own childhood and now they were mine also. But now it was Tupac, Cypress Hill and Wu Tang. Did you ever listen to some of those lyrics? People would slag off NWA because of their Fuck The Police track - just because of those three words. But did they ever listen to the track properly? I don't know maybe because of my upbringing and background, and that of my mother, I identified with the hip hop culture. I sure as hell LOVED the beats. It isn't the same these days but then nothing is the same these days.

"I'm gonna dance, anyone coming up with me?" I knew even before I made the announcement exactly who would come up. Candice could never refuse a dance and in fairness to her, she knew how to bust the moves. She was tall and wiry and for some reason every one of her moves was emphasised and every one of them drew eyes to her, and to me. Myself, I was more conservative in the way I glided round the dance floor. I was very precise, very in rhythm and very with the beat, but there were no windmilling arms and high kicks from me. I always teased myself, secretly, that I didn't need to do too much work on that floor to be noticed. I just didn't. And this was true. Here it was more true than at any other time. I don't know what it was about the Rihanna and DJ Khalid track Wild Thoughts. Was it the soaring guitar riffs between versus or was it the super cool dulcet tones of Rhianna. In the video version of that track she does this little 'shimmie' through one of those exotic out door clubs. That was what I was doing now. Ha ha the white girl in stilettos and Lycra trying to be the super cool black chick. I know I know, it didn't quite ring true, did it? But I was having a good time and that was what counted. Fuck the world - the wine and the cocktails had hit the spot.

"Hey you, would you like to join us for a drink. We haven't been able to take our eyes off you." That was that woman again. Me and Candice were just leaving the dance floor after 'that' track and this woman rubbed shoulders with me. I'm not sure if alarm bells should have been ringing at this time or not. I guess when I think about it now, yes alarm bells should have been sounded. Being told how amazing I looked by a woman, and man maybe in passing was one thing. But being told that they couldn't keep their eyes off me maybe was something that should have at least made me frown. The fact was that it didn't. I could just feel myself smiling. Smiling wide. I kind of liked the fact that they couldn't take their eyes off me. Mum would be proud to say the least. I giggled to myself when I thought about mum. Yes, she would be proud. She wouldn't be quite so proud of me now though. What she would feel now, well, I don't know. Well, to be mysterious, I do know what she would think and feel, but at the same time I didn't.

"Why not, sure." And I smiled at the woman again. Looking back, she was in my personal space a little bit. I was more than aware of her womanhood. She was dressed a little older than me, obviously, not very 'club' at all. I was quite tall at five feet nine, even more so in those heels. But she was taller. And she was more maturely built. Curvier, bust heavy. But, yes, she was in my space a bit. But that didn't ring alarm bells either because it was the club. It was crowded and tight and people tended to invade other people's spaces. I could smell her perfume. It was expensive, I could tell that. And then there was the way her warm breath rushed over my face when she spoke. Strangely the handsome, BIG, suited man stood back. He was looking but he stood back. I could feel his eyes on me, but I was used to that and he was standing back, so that was ok. I have to say that this couple didn't make me feel uncomfortable at all. They just didn't. Maybe my fearlessness was something that followed me through from childhood. Maybe that was more of my 'street' coming through.

Candice whispered to me "Are you sure about this? I mean you don't know them." Maybe the alarm bells had rung in her head. Maybe she should have shared more of her thoughts instead of the obvious. I don't know. "I'll be fine it's just a few tables away. Promise I'll behave." And we laughed. She was happy with how I felt about the situation and like I had said, I would be just a few tables away. What I didn't think about at the time was the skilful way this couple, or more precisely the woman herself had excluded Candice from the invite. I mean we were together. We were leaving the dance floor together and yet the invite to join the couple for a drink had only come to me. And there was nothing said that excluded Candice. It was just a 'thing' that the invite had been for me and me only.

When I got to the table of the couple the drinks were already there. Champagne on ice. I wasn't used to champagne but it did make me feel kind of good that these people had seen me worthy enough to order a bottle of bubbly. "Ohhhh champers. I do love a good

27

champers." I was lying. I hated the stuff. I hated the bubbles and I hated the taste. Fucking awful if I am honest with myself. And to be able to taste the difference between the cheap stuff and the expensive stuff was just way over my head. We sat and I just said, "thank you for the invite, although, I'm not entirely sure why. I mean this place is full of gorgeous girls, and yet you invite me." Maybe those alarm bells had rung on a sub level or something. It was a fair question. "Oh for sure there are lots of gorgeous girls here but not ones like you." And this woman just seemed to know what to say to put me at ease. And at the same time she just touched my arm lightly.

There was a little bit of quiet, or non-talking when we sipped the bubbly. Yuck! But I smiled and made like I enjoyed it. I was polite, always polite. The woman sat next to me, the man opposite me. I don't know what it was. It was like being in this little bubble at this table. Everything, the club was outside it, and we were in it. I glanced across and there were the girls getting on with their night. Every so often one or the other of them would look across at me. Kind of making sure I was ok. Those looks got less and less the more time that passed. It was like they had checked out this couple and decided they were harmless. Maybe Candice had decided that they were a little odd, but the last time that our eyes met, she smiled wide. It was one of her complete and wide smiles. I knew she was ok with things when I saw that smile.

"I'll just bet your mom helps you get ready, right?" It was a strange thing for this woman to say. And it was out of the blue. But I couldn't deny it - mum did help me. She influenced me a great deal. "Oh, and by the way, I'm Geena and this is Rob." The introductions - they came kind of late and even then, it was like they were second thoughts. She extended her hand and just for a second I looked at it. Then I placed mine in hers. "Pleased to meet you both. I'm Tara. I could kill my mum for calling me that, but what can I do." And I said that with a wide smile. Like an affectionate smile so that these people knew that I was joking about killing my mum. "That's just nonsense. Tara is a beautiful name. Beautiful name for a beautiful girl. And you most certainly are a beautiful girl." This time I was aware that she was touching my leg under the table. I could feel my eyes widen at first. But I thought it was ok. She was just getting over her point. But she kept her hand there. It was just resting on my upper thigh. The dress I had on was so short that it didn't cover that part of my crossed over leg, so her hand, her fingers were on the sheer nylon of my pantyhose.

"Oh, and by the way, yes my mum ALWAYS helps me get dressed for going out. She always has. We just have a giggle when we do it." I don't know, maybe I should have casually slipped her hand off my thigh. Let it be known that I didn't want it to be there. But if I am honest I didn't really mind. Ok it was a bit forward of her to put her hand right there and keep it there. If it had been a brush or a slight touch and then taken away then that would have been ok. And yet this wasn't bad. Maybe this was just one of those touchy-feely women who couldn't help but to 'touch'. There was this 'warmth of her hand through the nylon of the hose and that wasn't that unpleasant. And then there was the slight movement of the fingers. Not a lot. Just really as though she was letting me know that her hand was still there.

"I'm sure she does. And I have to say that she does a fabulous job. You look breath-taking." This woman was full of compliments and I can't say that what she was saying was making me feel bad because it wasn't. In fact, quite the opposite. It was like what mum had said about making people want you, and how to look in heels and

29

makeup and all of that stuff, this was proof of the pudding. Except that this wasn't some creep of a man coming on to me. This was a seemingly nice couple who were just, it seemed, saying it as it was. Still that hand stayed there, and that movement of the fingers was still there. I had thought maybe for some weird fucked up reason she was testing me. Seeing if I said anything. That was what I was thinking. That she was testing me. I didn't know what for. Maybe just a weird thing. To me everything was weird back then. I was a teenager for fucks sakes. I didn't need an explanation in minute detail for everything that went on. Things happened, shit happened, shit happens.

And this was just another thing that was happening. And the thing was it wasn't unpleasant. She wasn't groping me. Or being nasty. There was just this warmth, and this 'nice' thing going on. Looking back now, she was testing me. I know that now. And the thing was that the longer it went on - the longer it went without me doing anything or saying anything about her constantly shifting fingers on my nylon sheathed thigh, the deeper in it I got. The longer it went on the less likely I was to say anything or do anything. It was like this woman had made some sort of move on me and now that she had done that and now that her move had been established under the table, it was less and less likely that I would stop it. And that was the sign that she needed to progress things further.

I was more than aware of the man watching across the table. He had this intense stare. He hadn't said a word. I have to say in my defence, not that I had to defend myself against anything that these things happened so quickly. I was so taken aback to feel those fingers and that palm on my leg that I was speechless to that if I am honest. And then the intense stare of the man. It was almost like he had his hand on my leg and was looking at me, studying me for any kind of reaction. It was more like he knew that the Geena's hand was on my leg. Like he absolutely knew that it was there and he was daring me to saying something or do something. I can't deny that this was a weird thing. It was something that didn't faze me initially. It didn't faze me at all really because the sensation, and the feel of Geena's hand there, right there was not unpleasant. In fact, it was more than nice.

Yes, I was aware of the creep of Geena's hand up my thigh. She was just sliding her whole flat hand, and her fingers up higher then taking them back down. And then higher again, higher than the last time and then back again so that the overall progress was a slow one but one that I was aware of. I looked over the table with the girls on it but they were having a laugh. There were no eyes on me at all. That was ok. I didn't feel in danger or anything. Like I said there were no alarm bells. In fact, I was beginning to think this was a bit of an adventure. I was curious more than anything. If this woman was feeling my leg like this - and it was suggestively, what exactly was she suggesting? I'm not sure at what stage it became 'sexual' for me. When I think now, it was certainly sexual for this couple then. But I don't know at what point it became sexual for me. I mean by this time in my life I knew about sex. I even knew about masturbation. And I knew the value of what I looked like and how I carried myself and how I came across to others. I had got all of that from my mother. She had taught me well. But I wasn't sure about this night and when it became a sexual thing. I think it was simply that things moved with fluidity and a smoothness. There was no dividing line between non-sexual and sexual. It was all as one.

"Well, this is pleasant. Isn't it?" It was the way Geena spoke. There was a tone to her voice, a different

31

tone to her voice that I hadn't heard before. And she was looking right at me. I mean she had turned her head and she was looking directly at me, and her eyes were drilling me. It was like she had asked a question that she wanted an answer to. The thing was that the club by this time was in full swing. It was going for it. There was the thump thump thump of the base and I could hear that coming up through the arch of my feet in the stilettos. And yet at the same time there was the bubble of this table that we were sitting at. I looked over to the girls table just briefly. A couple of them had gone already. I looked at my watch. Fuck time was flying! "Yes, yes this is nice." It was all I could think of to say. I pressed my red lips together and rolled them in. I did that sometimes when I was in certain situations. Like awkward situations.

And Geena just held my gaze and I could feel myself blush because it was like she knew about my wetness down there. Her hand had been up and down my thigh so many times over such a length of time that she must have felt it for herself. I felt so ashamed of myself even though she didn't say anything. She might not even have known. But that wasn't the point. She might have known and that WAS the point. Besides, she had changed what she was doing with her fingers. She was using her nails and she was lightly scratching me through the nylon. That was a strange feeling. A strange sensation like a 'scritching' through the sheerness of the nylon. It was like a tickle but not a tickle at the same time. Geena wasn't pressing her nails in hard. She was using them softly if that makes sense. It was like a sensuous thing and something that she knew how to do well.

"It's ok sweetheart. Just relax. Relax and go with it." And her voice - I don't know it just changed over time. She moved her chair closer to me and once again she was in my space. I got that aroma of her perfume and that seemed to work with the champagne and make me all heady and dreamy. By the time she was scritching her nails through my panty crotch and through the nylon I know now it was 'pleasure' that I was feeling. It felt as though I had come alive down there. And more than that - the wetness had increased. At one point Geena took her fingers away from me and held them up. Showing me her finger dripping with juice that had filtered and squeezed through my pantyhose and the crotch of the panties. I blushed again. And this time the man, Rob, he was leaned over the table and he was looking right into my eyes. And the thing about that was that it was a deliberate invasion of my space. They were both invading my space. And yet still this man hadn't uttered a single word to me. I was beginning to wonder if he was a mute or something. Later, much later I would label him Rob the mute.

"Take your panties off honey, there's a good girl." Geena's instruction was casual. Not like she was saying anything overtly sexual at all. And now it had become like that I swallowed dryly. I looked across at the table again with the girls on it. I must have timed it right because Candice was looking right at me and she was smiling widely. I smiled back but wasn't sure that my smile was my normal one. There was too much going on in my head, and in other places. They weren't concerned about me obviously. I wasn't concerned about me. I was just a little worried that I was enjoying what Geena was doing to me under the table. I gasped when she slipped her dripping finger into her mouth and sucked it clean. She was tasting me. She was tasting me in front of me. My blush deepened I could feel it. "Panties Tara, now." And there was that change in voice again and in tone. Geena was, I don't know, she was getting into my head. I wriggled on the seat and looked around as though

33

waiting to spot someone who had spotted what I was doing. There wasn't anyone of course. Just me wriggling out of my panties. Rolling them down my thighs and then down over my knees and then lifting one stilettoed foot and then the other removing them.

I didn't quite know what to do with my panties. I had them in my hand all damp and squishy with the damp. That made me feel more ashamed. But Geena helped with that. She took her little bag up onto the table and she opened it up. She didn't say anything - she just looked at me, then the panties and then her bag. I reached across and slipped my panties into her bag and she closed it.

Chapter 4

I'm not sure how I felt when I saw Geena closing her bag with my panties in it. It was strange. I swallowed dryly again. For some reason I couldn't look at her. I had no problem looking at her before. There was nothing before that bothered me. But it had all changed by the time I removed my panties like that. Like before the sexuality was only hinted at. Ok it might have been hinted at in the way I was dressed and made up - like an unspoken overt sexuality. But now it was as though some kind of line had been crossed. The line had been stepped on when Geena had told me to remove my panties. And that was another thing. She had 'told' me to do it. I was having a bit of an issue knowing that I had done as I was told. Only my mum ever told me what to do, and that was getting less and less as I got older. And yet here was this woman telling me what to do in a sexual way. And that was something that I was having trouble coming to terms with. That was why I couldn't look at her. That line stepped on and now crossed with me removing my panties and slipping them into this woman's bag. I was wondering was I some kind of disgusting bitch for doing that? I didn't think it at the time - not at the exact time that I slipped those panties off and into her bag. But it was the kind of thing that weighed a little bit heavy on my mind after the fact. That was why I couldn't look at her. Or him. I couldn't look at him either.

I didn't mean to let out the deep, groan when Geena moved her hand back to my leg. It was that scritching though. I don't know what it was about it. It just sent all kinds of sensations up into my sexuality. I still couldn't look at her though. I kept my head down. I was grateful that she didn't give me another instruction that I had to follow. The one where she told me to look at her as she did what she was doing. Thank god she didn't give me that one. But that scritching of the nylon. That was just weird and it was beautiful at the same time. And the thing was that Geena had moved her hand up higher. I remember thinking that she had no right to assume that I wouldn't ask her to stop. But that thought was immediately put on hold. It was the way she did it - it was the way it felt like she had every right to do that. And the groan, the deep wet groan came when her nail, the perfectly manicured polish nail 'scritched' my sex lips through the nylon. That was something that I had never felt before. That was something that I had never experienced before. The way she did it, weighting it perfectly. Pressing her nail but not hard, just enough to indent each lip in turn and tracing the puffy swell of my lips one at a time. First up one and then down the other. And her doing it in quick succession. Down one, up the other, and then down the middle of the both of them. I gulped and then let out that groan.

I wasn't sure if the sound of the groan carried or not. The club was noisy, I was pretty certain that it didn't carry. I looked over the table with the girls on but there was only Frankie and Candice left now and they were busy talking. I wondered if they looked over would they see me in some kind of quandary and come and get me out of it. I kind of wished that would happen but at the same time didn't want it to happen because of the nice feeling I was getting from Geena's finger nail. She kept her finger pressed in at the top of my nylon sheathed slit. It was my clitoris that she had her finger nail pressed in to. She wasn't moving her finger but she was just altering the angle of it. Pressing it and in doing that moving the clitoris. Using the wet from my cunt, the wetness oozing through the sheer nylon of the pantyhose. Fuck, I don't know why but knowing that I was wet like this and knowing that I was enjoying what she was doing like

36

this, I was feeling really ashamed of myself. I never thought much about the words slut and whore and all those kind of derogatory words but now they were coming to me like flashes in my mind. It was at this point I kind of understood the way men and boys used those words. And that those words were kind of appropriate to me in this place at this time.

Then there was the man, Rob. He was looking at me. I wasn't looking up but I could feel him looking at me. I didn't want to look up. I didn't want to look at either of them so I didn't. I kept my head down. I just kept looking at the top of the table. I could have moved away from Geena. I could have got up and walked away. I wouldn't have created a scene - I could have just got up and walked away but I didn't. I should have. I know now I should have. God only knows now that I should have walked away. But I didn't do that. I stayed there because what this woman was doing to me between the legs was so nice. It was so something that I hadn't, it was so something that I didn't want to end that I stayed there. I even opened my legs a little bit more for Geena. I could feel myself blushing a furious red under all of that makeup. But I stayed there because I didn't want that beautiful feeling between my legs to stop. I wanted it to go on and on and on. And now I could especially feel Rob's eyes drilling into me. It would have been so easy to flick my eyes up to meet his but I didn't do that. I couldn't.

I could just feel his eyes, and hers on me. And now she was working my lips through the nylon in a much more animated way. She was walking her fingers up and down my slit. It was odd that she was doing that. It was odd because in doing what she was doing she was 'owning' the sexual flesh she was walking her fingers up and down. "You're enjoying this aren't you Tara?" That voice, her voice filtering in to my head and psyche. I just half nodded and half grunted but I kept my eyes down to the table top. "I didn't quite get that, and look at me when you speak Tara - don't be rude. I said, you're enjoying this aren't you Tara?" And that was the worst thing in the world to me. That she had told me to look at her. I could have answered still with my eyes cast down to the table top. But now that wasn't an option. That really was the worse time of my life. Those few seconds. That instruction being given and me knowing that I had to do as I was told. What was escaping me at this time was that I didn't have to do what I was told. I could still simply get up from that table and walk away. But that as an option was not even in my head. All that was in my head was that I had to do as I was told. All that was there was there was them and me and the knowledge that I was with them, doing what they wanted and I couldn't walk away. I would regret not walking away eventually. Regret it from the bottom of my soul.

"Yes, yes I am enjoying it. Yes I am." And I was looking right at Geena. I was mortified and it must have shown on my face. She was still working her fingers but her eyes were locked on mine. It was about this time that Candice appeared at the table. She was completely oblivious to what was happening under the table or with my state of mind. She had absolutely no idea of my plight. Both her and Frankie were all the worse for the drink by now. "We're going to hit the road Tara. You coming with us, or staying for a while?" She flicked her eyes between me, Geena and Rob.

Fact is that she would have had to be stone cold sober to have been able to see anything amiss. "Oh you know sweetie, we'll make sure Tara gets to where she needs to be, isn't that right Tara?" Geena had taken the question and owned it. In a way I was grateful for that because I wasn't sure that I would have been able to come out with anything other than another one of those wet, drizzling groans. When Candice looked at me I just mouthed "Yeah I'll be ok. I'll catch you tomorrow." And at the same time Geena was pushing the nylon inside between my sex lips and she was using the sheer coarseness of it to produce more and more sensations that were starting to blow my mind. I knew that I should have gone with Candice. But at the same time I knew that I couldn't leave these sensations behind.

I could feel Geena's finger inside me, and that nylon. And I could feel it all slippery down there, inside me - and that wetness oozing out of me. I was aware of Candice just backing off and going. She was a sensible girl so she can't have been worried about me. There can have been nothing happening that would have looked odd to her - or would have told her that I was in any form of danger. She must have been happy that I was ok and that this couple were safe for me to be with. I could have said something. I should have but I didn't want that pleasure down there to stop. I wanted it to go on and on and on. "Wave your friends off Tara. You're going to be just fine with us. You're going to be just fine." There was some change in Geena's voice. Maybe it was me I don't know. She was in close to me now and she was whispering but she was smiling at the same time. I looked over at Candice. She was just about to leave but her eye caught mine and I waved to her. She wouldn't have been able to see my hand trembling as I waved it. I could though. Geena was sending that sensation through me and it was making me shake. I don't know - somehow she had changed the way she was doing it. The finger was still poking the nylon inside me and it was more wet down there now. It was more slippery and it was easier for Geena to do what she was doing.

Actually, it was like she was doing what she was doing casually and with hardly any effort. And now she was involving the softer folds of flesh inside me. Mixing the fine nylon of my pantyhose and her finger and finger nail with the saturated swamp like wetness of my inner sex flesh. I could feel myself shuddering down the core of the spine. Candice and Frankie were gone now. I could see them, just vanishing through the doors to the front of the club. The crowd was thinning now and the night was coming to an end. I had this weird feeling, this weird 'need' in that I didn't want the night to end. I didn't want the night to end and I didn't want to move or shift on the chair too much. I didn't want to disturb Geena's finger, or the movement of the finger in me because I was afraid if I did that sensation would stop and it wouldn't come back. I was aware that I was being quite irrational. But not irrational in the way I was acting. I mean irrational inside my head. Worried about losing that sensation from that finger for fucks sakes. What was the matter with me? I ran my tongue across the underside of my top lip as I saw Frankie vanish through that door. Candice had already gone. I was on my own now.

That was something that did strike me. That I was on my own. But even at this time I did not feel any danger. I just didn't feel any danger. I was with another woman for gods sakes! That had to be a good thing. If it had just been the mysterious man of few words Rob, then I am sure that the alarm bells would have been ringing by now. He didn't say anything, he just looked. He just had that intense stare going on - all the time. It wasn't just that he had these periods of staring. He did it all the time. I don't know maybe it was because of that that I felt like I was on some kind of edge all the time. Maybe that was it. To be honest it didn't matter to me. I just didn't want Geena to take her finger or the nylon out of me. It was odd, the deeper she poked in that nylon the deeper I wanted her to go with it. And when she had poked right in, the way she moved her finger inside me, involving all of the folds of flesh.

She was involving all of the folds of flesh and all of the depths of flesh. The whole of my slit had become a swamp. A wet hot swamp. "I'd like to take you home with us Tara. You'd like that wouldn't you?" I swallowed another spasm of that pure pleasure that she was giving me. Of course I should have said no. Of course I should have put a stop to this madness now. I know NOW that I should have done that. But at that time, I was on an adventure. My first real sexual adventure and I was having the time of my life. I just nodded, "Mmmm yes, yes I'd like that. Thank you." What was I thanking her for? But I meant it, I would like it. I wanted to go home with them. I didn't care. It meant that she wanted to do other things to me. Give me other pleasure. I was more than up for it. I felt as though I was desperate for it. Nothing would have stopped me going with Geena and Rob that night, nothing!

What was there not to like? Then there was the 'rip' of Geena's nail going through the crotch of my pantyhose. Even that rip, even that sensations sent pleasure through me that I cannot describe. It was pure pleasure. It was like Geena had worked me in such a way that I was so sensitive, so utterly sensitive to everything thing that she did down there that I could 'feel' that rip. It seemed to reverberate up and down the length of my slit. My outer lips caught it and so did the inner folds of flesh. The fluid, the oily slippery fluid that was oozing from me seemed to act as a conductor to the ripping of that nylon. The pleasure seemed to swim through the fluid and it seemed to be amplified through that fluid. Geena wasn't having to do very much to make that pleasure happen. I'm sure when I look back to that night that this pleasure was more because it was in my head. I was soaking up the physical pleasure of having those sexual nerves toyed with, but my head was doing the rest. And now Geena's fingers, not one but several, were dancing all over my naked, exposed sex flesh. Now there was no nylon. She had ripped a gaping hole in the crotch of my pantyhose. And it was like, now that she had done that, she was announcing that she had the free run of my sex flesh. That she could and would do whatever she wanted to and how she wanted to and there was nothing that I could do about it. At least that was how my mind was processing it.

I don't know why I was putting it all together in my mind like that. But that was what was happening. I was starting to have these outlandish fantasies as she worked her fingers across and inside my sexuality under that table. "Gonna be a good girl for me Tara?" That was another hissing, whispering thing that she fed into one of my ears. At first I didn't understand the question and then I decided that if it meant me getting this pleasure then yes, I would be a good girl. Whatever being a good girl meant. My mum used to say that to me. Good girl! And are you going to be a good girl for mum? But that usually meant when something was going to happen that wasn't particularly nice or pleasant. Like a visit to the dentist, or the doctors. This wasn't like that. I found it easy to dribble out the answer from between my lips. "Mmm yes, yes of course I'll be a good girl for you, of course." And I meant it. As I was answering and as all sorts of stuff was going through my mind, Geena was working her fingers in another different way. She had them deep inside me, I could feel them deep. And she was hooking them up and back. And that was when another form of pleasure hit me. A huge hit of absolute, but different pleasure.

I know now that what Geena had done was locate my G spot. And what she was doing was rubbing the flesh of my G spot with her wet slippery fingers. The pleasure was instant and it was a pleasure that stayed as long as those fingers were touching the slight rougher flesh of the G spot. I could feel my oral lips trembling but at the same time I could feel Geena's warm breath washing over my face. She was so close to me by this time. She was in my personal space but I didn't mind that. In fact I wanted it. "Soon, we're just going to walk out of here, the three of us and you're going to be smiling for me aren't you Tara. If you smile when we leave, make like everything is fine, then you can have some more of this pleasure when we get back to the house. How does that sound, is that a deal?" In a way she was telling me that things weren't alright or why would I have to smile as though it was? That didn't make sense and that did cross my mind but I didn't care. To be honest I wasn't in a state of mind to analyse the words that Geena was using properly. If I had been, I would have made a run for it maybe. Or not.

Even as Geena's words were sinking in she was using her fingers across and round my G spot. Round and round. And at the same time she was sinking her fingers deep into me, making my sex flesh, my deeper sex flesh react by gripping those fingers as though it had a life of its own. "It's, it's a deal." I stuttered more in a gasp than anything. I didn't want Geena to take those fingers out of me. In the event though, when she did, I wanted to get out of this place - out of the club and get back to wherever the house was. I have to say that at this point I was a willing party to what was happening. This woman had given and shown me pleasure that I could never have imagined and now I wanted some more of that. I think perhaps it was a selfishness in me that was driving me. I smiled - just like I had been told to do. And I left with this couple.

Chapter 5

I can just about remember leaving that club. It wasn't that I just about remembered it, it was more that I could 'just' see through the sexual haze that I was in when we left. I remembered the instructions for me to smile and I was smiling. I had the feeling that it was more of a grimace that I was producing with my red lips. A grimace that might tell anyone in the know that I had more on my mind than the way I looked. The way I felt that was it. I was so needy and the high heels were making me walk, making me strut in a slow sensuous way. It was as though my sexuality was trying to find 'the' walk, the strut that would cause some movement down there between my legs. The ripped panty hose crotch meant that I could feel wisps of fresh air around my crotch. That made me suck in air. But I found that if I walked with that supermodel type deliberateness, scissoring my legs and taking long strides, that I could get the movement down there that I needed. That was it. The one foot in front of the other. Purposeful lady like strides. Except what those strides were doing to me weren't ladylike.

As we made our way through the remaining crowd I was having to twist this way and the next and that was adding to the sense of over-sexuality that I was feeling. It was making me needy. It was funny really - everything just became sexual. The slightest move, the different steps, the way I twisted to get past someone. And I was aware of the man Rob and the woman Geena either side of me. They were pressed in slightly - as though they were guiding me. As though they didn't want me to take a wrong turn. Or to get lost in the throng of people now filtering out of the club. Looking back, they were on a mission to get me out of the club that night. It was as though they had reached a critical time in their plan and that they couldn't afford for anything to go wrong - or for me to go AWOL.

There was a car waiting but I didn't take much notice of it. A huge limousine type car. I remember just sniggering to myself slightly. I'd never been for a ride in a limousine before. I did question myself about that. Like who are these people? Why would these people who had their own driver be spending time in that type of club when they did, if the truth be known, stand out in the crowd? Truth was that at that time, I had had my mind blown in such a way that I didn't care about the answers to mundane questions. There was more to explore with these people than who they were and why they were where they were. Looking back now I know that I was in the frame of mind that I was supposed to be in. That I was in the head space that this couple needed me to be in. Rob hadn't said a word to me, not one word all night. There had been times when he had leaned into Geena and seemed to whisper something. But he had barely even acknowledged me except for that intense, intense stare. I knew for sure I existed in his world because of that stare. But that was about it.

And now in the big car it was the same. I was sitting between the two of them, like I was trapped between the two of them. It didn't matter. Even that feeling of being trapped between them was an added feel to my sexuality. It wasn't unpleasant sitting in this car between these two people like this. Truth be known all I could think of was my own pleasure. I know now that was selfish. If I hadn't been so selfish then I might have heard those distant alarm bells. Except there were no alarm bells. There were none at all. Just a needy me, and these two people. Rob even before we set off in the car had draped his lower arm and hand over one of my thighs. That had been like a small shock to the system. It shouldn't have been but it was. The sexual stall had been laid out.

Geena had done what she did to me in the club and there was an undeniable sexual element between us all. Maybe I should have swiped Rob's hand off. But the way he had done it. The way he had just draped his arm and hand like that, was like he had every right to do that. And then I remembered what Geena had said about me being a good girl. I could live with that arm and hand. I could even live with the little scritching motions his fingers were doing with was left of the pantyhose nylon on the inside of my upper thigh.

Geena did the same. There had been that little period of adjustment and then her hand had crept onto my thigh. She smoothed her flat palm and then she curled her fingers a little bit and there was that 'scritching' again. I don't know why. I thought that even in the car that one thing would lead to another and before very long that the two of them would be at my sex flesh. That they would be doing things to my sex flesh that would feed me more and more. But it didn't happen like that. It was as though the contact with their arms and hands from either side of my, to my upper thighs was exactly what they intended. It was like they were just keeping me fed, just keeping me needy enough. It was like there was always that 'possibility', that there was always that thought that something more dirty would happen in the back of that car. And again, of the truth was known that was what I wanted. It was what I needed - for something dirty and slippery to happen. But it didn't.

I'm more than sure that I was salivating profusely as the car glided out into the early morning traffic. It was still dark but the sun would be rising soon. In a moment, a split second of clarity I spoke, "I should call my mum, let her know I'll be late." I wasn't watching the direction of travel or where we were going. There was this like separation between what was happening outside the car

46

and what was happening inside. "Oh, don't you worry about that sweetie. We'll do it when we get back to the house. Don't you worry about a thing. All you need to worry about is how much of a good girl you're going to be for us." Yes, I know, I know that was another point at which the alarm bells should have rung. There was something more than creepy about the way that Geena spoke in the car. And then there was the fact that Rob hadn't said a word. Not a word, and ye there he was with his arm draped over my leg and his fingers doing that thing they were doing. I didn't care. I even believed Geena when she told me not to worry. I wasn't worried. I was a big girl and mum knew that I was growing up and spreading my wings. There was this thing in my mind that was telling me that mum knew I was spreading my wings not my legs. And that was what I was doing, in that car. I was opening my legs against those of Rob and Geena. I guess I was just letting them know that I was up and willing for anything.

I didn't have a clue that they already knew what I was up for. I didn't have a clue that they were working me and that in that car I was where they needed me to be and that I was in the right frame of mind for what they wanted. When the car eventually went through the electronic gates of a huge detached house and then down a ramp into an underground carpark, I didn't have a clue where I was. I didn't know how long the car ride had been. I had no idea of the direction that we had travelled. I knew nothing, literally nothing. But you know, I didn't care. All I cared about were the throbs that seemed to be pulsating from between my legs. When we got out of the car it was a little more relaxed. I had a little more space to myself. It was like at the club and outside, the couple had had to shepherd me and guide me and make sure that I didn't speak to anyone. Or more, that I didn't say the wrong thing to anyone. But now that I was back in their domain. Now I was in their space and in their comfort zone, there was a little bit more of a relaxed feel to it. I felt that but I didn't know why I felt it. I guess yet again it was an alarm bell that I missed, or didn't hear. Maybe I didn't hear it because it wasn't there. We were back at this huge house now, and I was hoping this woman, and even this man would show me some more of that ultra pleasure that she had shown me in the club.

Of course I know now that it was all part of the plan. All part of a minutely orchestrated plan to bring me down. Even now, I don't get why they had to do this to me. They could have had anything that night. They could have had their own pleasure any way they wanted it and I would have been up for it. I would have let them just because I wanted and needed it so much. I just didn't get why they had to do this to me. All of this. They took me up into the house via an elevator. It was a very posh, very big house. An immaculate house. Even in my needy dripping state I remember thinking how immaculate this house was. And how everything was in its place and how there was a place for everything. The touches to my sexuality hadn't happened in the car. I know now that was deliberate. Deliberate to make me needy the way I was. But at least we were back at the house now and at least this couple could get on with it. I was reasoning with myself, or trying to, that they wouldn't have gone to all this trouble to take me back to this place if they weren't going to have amazing sex with me. It just stood to reason, at least to me that they would not do that.

In a way my reasoning was right. But what I wasn't getting at that time was that this was a couple who would do things on their own terms. That anything that happened, happened for them. Not for me but for them! I knew that as I sat on the high-backed chair with the dress off my shoulder and my breasts just out there. Geena had been very specific when she told me, "Sit Tara, lower your dress and expose your breasts for Us." And she had emphasised the Us. If I am honest that was kind of creepy. Ok they could enjoy what they did to me, but with what I was feeling between my legs, the hot slipperiness, surely they were doing it for me? No they weren't. My pleasure wasn't the objective at all. At least not my orgasmic pleasure. They were not about to gratify me and let me go on my merry way. I know that now. I didn't know it then though. I knew that my nostrils were flaring because of this need I had in me. Even as I sat like that I wanted something to happen down there. That was because they knew what I would be wanting. Or not so much knew what I wanted but knowing that I needed something to be happening. Something, anything.

"You're very needy aren't you Tara?" It was the first time I had heard that needy word. And yet I knew immediately that it was what I felt. "I am yes, I'm sorry." I thought if I admit it they would get on with it. I was sure that whatever happened this night I would not be sharing it with mum. I had made up my mind about that even at this point. With the way things panned out, I'd never be able to willingly share with mum ever again. Not willingly! That was the operative word, willingly. I didn't know why I apologised for being needy. They had made me like it. I'm sure it was my inexperience and some kind of guilt that was sliding into my psyche I'm not sure. That I was sat in front of this wine sipping couple exposed the way I was and knowing how wet I was down there. And how stiff my nipples had become. "No need to apologise Tara - you are what you are." And there was innuendo in what Geena said. I am what I am! What did that even mean I didn't know? Little subtle things being said that were putting me in my place. It makes more sense to me now than it did then. It makes perfect sense to me now that they, or more particular that

49

she had to treat me the way she treated me so that I would be prepared for what would happen to me.

"Let's slide that dress of your up over your hips Tara, and then sit with your legs spread wide. You don't need to be ashamed to expose how needy you are. Like I said you are what you are." And there it was again, the innuendo. I didn't need to be ashamed which meant that shame was being fed into my psyche and all because I was what I was. I didn't know then what that meant. I know and understand more now. I won't pretend that I know everything, or that I understand everything because I don't. What I have been through is a complete mind and body fuck. But I kind of understand now that girls like me need this in their lives. Whatever the fuck 'this' is. I did it. I slid up the micro dress around my hips - and with it being off my shoulder, it was like a belt around my middle. And I placed my stilettos wide apart and spread my knees. This was ok for me because it was as though now I would get that pleasure that I needed all over again. But that shame that I needn't have had - it was there.

And then the feeling that I wasn't the same as other girls because of how needy I was - that was there as well. And I could feel myself like a warm slippery swamp down there. And now there were no panties and no pantyhose crotch there to hide the state of me down there. That was the thing - that I was exposed. I felt exposed and I felt that this couple, the odd couple knew everything about me. I didn't get that if I'm honest. I didn't get that this couple who I had met only hours ago could know about me. Not all about me. The man hadn't said a word to me. How could he know about me? And the woman Geena, she had only complimented me and then set about bringing me to their table where she had kind of sexually molested me. She didn't know me. She didn't know me at all.

50

There was a bit of resentment in me, I could feel it. But the needy wanting slut in me was winning through. I did get the micro flashbacks and thoughts of mum. And when that happened there was this guilt that washed over me. It didn't change the way I sat or exposed myself for this couple because I still had that need. I still needed to revisit the pleasure that I had felt in the club when Geena was doing that thing between my legs. When I think back now, I was a young girl with an older experienced couple. What was I thinking? I know the answer to that, and again it's between my legs. If I really try to analyse what happened that night I can't. Was it my real sexual awakening? Was it an adventure I had to see through to the end? Or was it all about this couple who had spotted me and then set about bringing me into their world in preparation for what they would do to me. I know the answer to that now too. But it's too late now. What I didn't know was that the process had begun a long time ago. Years ago, in fact. But how could I know that?

Geena stroking my breasts but not touching my nipples was like some kind of torment. I wish I could describe the torment. I know NOW what real torment is but I thought that this was it. Geena just stroking my breasts very softly, very sensuously. "Just hold your hands behind the back of the chair Tara - you'll feel what I'm doing better then. You'll feel it much, much better." I don't know if it was the power of suggestion or what - but I did feel it better. It was a much better feeling when I slipped my hands to the back of the chair. It was as though I was thrusting out my breasts for her to touch and stroke. I could feel every nuanced stroke. Every little move with her individual fingers.

Everything, I could feel it. But what I needed most was for her to touch my nipples. For her to include my stiff thick nipples in her strokes but she didn't do that. She did everything but that. And it was like she knew what I wanted and what I needed. "You want me to touch them don't you Tara?" and as she was talking she was just circling my nipples. First one then the other. She was just circling them outside the speckled darker aureole. She could have touched them she could have run the pad of her finger tip over the nipple tip, because if she had then I would have felt the reverberation down at my clitoris. You know, that invisible string that connects the clitoris with the nipples? But she didn't do that and I know that she didn't do it deliberately. Part of me felt that Geena was a bitch for teasing me in this way. But I couldn't do anything about that. I didn't even want to do anything about it.

That was what I felt that she was doing was teasing me. Un-mercilessly teasing me. More than that I felt that she was enjoying doing this to me. I could feel her eyes on me, as though studying me and the effects of what she was doing. And she was in my personal space again, right in it. I knew this because again I could feel the warmth of her breath washing over my face. But she never touched my nipples, not even accidentally. If anything, she was surgically precise in the way that she circled them. In the deliberate way that she avoided the nipple tips. I could feel myself oozing more between the legs and I could feel a solitary tear run down my cheek. But Geena spotted that and she caught it with one of her forefingers. She scooped it up and placed it on her tongue. That shouldn't have turned me on more, but it did. She was tasting me again. She had tasted me in the club and now she was tasting me again. Maybe this meant that I would get some more of that pleasure that I had felt before. I was so needy and by this time I must have looked as needy as I actually was. The thing was that the neediness, and the guilt were as one, and both of those states of mind, both of those states of being were working on me in unison.

Chapter 6

It was my fault that the man, Rob fucked me the way he did. I was so needy and so desperate that I would have done anything just to feel myself being penetrated. The thing was that I thought that I would go through the act and that everything would be ok after it. That I would feel better about it all and that life would go on. How could I have needed a man to fuck me so badly that I wouldn't even attempt to talk to him first? How could I be so drooling, so slippery wet inside my mind that I was pretty much begging for it? This was my age and my inexperience shining through. I was feeling the guilt. Geena had said, "ok, Rob will slip himself into you, but this is your fault Tara and don't try to make out that its anything else." And that had been Geena laying that guilt on me right at the start. As though she was taking time out. As though she was taking an interlude just to let this happen. Just to let Rob slip into me and ejaculate up inside me.

It was like she wanted this to happen so that she could then get on with the main event. As though she was prepared to let this happen but that it was all my fault. Not hers and not Rob's but mine. Of course I know now this was how it was supposed to feel. This was how it was supposed to happen. I was supposed to beg for it. And then I was supposed to get that guilt hit after it. Geena had teased me into some kind of complete and utter submission and when I begged for it, when I pleaded for some kind of release, that was far from unexpected. It was supposed to happen and it had happened on cue.

She had turned her attentions from my breasts back to my clitoris and she was edging me. I didn't know it was 'edging' then but I do now. I know all about edging now. She was touching and feeling and depressing my clitoris and she was doing that incessantly as I sat on that chair and she was simply bringing me to the point of orgasm time after time. I didn't even know it was orgasm that I was on the point of then. I know that now as well, only too well. She was simply bringing me to the point of 'something' that needed to be spilt over into something else. But instead of doing that she was bringing me to that first point and then she was altering her touch and feel and letting the intense feeling die back. And then she would wait for a little while, maybe seconds during which she would simply blow softly over my face - like a constant reminder of her presence and then she would begin with her fingers again and she would bring me right to that point again. This time she would take me further and further to that 'edge' - then she would stop.

I don't know how many times she did that - I didn't know how many times she brought me to that very edge. It was funny that I thought about it like that - me being on some kind of edge. Me being right there and then taken back. Each and every time it was like I was taken further and further to that precipice and then taken back. But each time it was more and more intense. Each time I let out some kind of wet, obscene groan. I'm sure it was obscene, that groan, it sure sounded like it to me. But I was in a place that I had never been in before. My head was a mess and my sexuality was oozing this oily slippery fluid out. More than once I almost grabbed Geena's hand and kept it pressed into me on the point that she took that edge away. But when I went to make the move she looked at me and I knew that I couldn't do that. I don't know why. She didn't say anything. She didn't tell me that I couldn't do it, or that I shouldn't do it. Or even that I would be in trouble if I did. She didn't say anything - she just looked and that was enough. In the end I was sobbing when she took that edge away from me. I hadn't been sobbing at the start, but by the time those edgings had been taken further and further all I did was sob.

"Would you like Rob to be inside you Tara? Its ok you can tell me. Our secret?" That had been like a pin prick to my senses that question. It was like a very tiny pinhole of light at the end of a very long tunnel. Did I really hear that? Did she mean what she was saying or was this another one of her cruel things that she did? "Yes, yes please. Please can Rob be inside me." I was pretty lucid, pretty aware of what was going on and so could hear the words I was saying. They were words that I would never have said. I would never sound like I was begging to be penetrated. I always had too much dignity for that to happen. But I was aware that that was what I sounded like. It sounded like I was begging - or at the very least it sounded as though I was desperate to be penetrated. It seemed like for a long time that Geena didn't say anything or do anything except swirl her fingers round in the honey pot that was my sex. In a way I wanted her to stop doing that. But I wanted her to carry on as well. She brought me to the edge again and I sobbed out. "Just tell me how much you'd like Rob inside you honey? I have to be sure that it's what you want and I am not completely convinced, not just yet."

Of course, I know now that she was playing with me. It was what she was doing on a massive scale. She was using the edgings and then her voice and her fingers to play with me and fuck me up a little bit more. As she took me all the way to that edge again it was like I was looking down into this huge open space - a black hole that wasn't black at all. She took me further this time and it felt like she might let me tumble into that next stage. It felt like she might let me orgasm. But that was another game that she played. That was another thing that she was doing with my mind. She took me there and then took me back again. And the thing was that just made

55

me more needy. It made me want Rob inside me even more. It could have been 'anyone' but that was another trick of the mind. It was only Rob 'on offer' so it was only Rob that I wanted inside me. It was only the mute man I wanted to feel slipping inside me. "Ohhhh I want it so much. So much I want to feel him in me, deep in me. Please can he be deep in me, please, please can he be deep in me." If there had been a question mark on whether I was begging before then that wasn't the case now. It wasn't just a begging it was a pleading. And it was from somewhere other than the heart.

I don't know what I expected. I don't know what I thought would happen when I begged like this. I didn't know what would happen if Geena agreed to Rob being inside of me. Did I think it would all be over and I would just be let go on my merry way? I just didn't know anything. My mind had been so mashed up with Geena edging me that thinking straight, or thinking logically was not something that I could do. More than once I had to suck my own drool back into my mouth. What I really needed was Geena to tip me over that edge that she brought me to time after time after time. But the only thing that seemed like a possibility was that Rob would slip his cock into me. I wasn't sure what would be better. I wasn't sure if I would be sated after either of the options. I didn't have a clue, I didn't have the slightest inclination that what I would get would simply leave me wanting more. I didn't have the slightest idea that being taken over that edge, and, or being taken by Rob would not leave me gratified or with a warm smile of contentment across my face at all. How could I know that I was being taken into a place, into a head space where the more I had, the more I would want? Like an addictive space inside my head and all melded with my sexuality. How could I have known that?

I was invited to sit on Rob's lap. Again, that was something that I would never have done in normal ordinary circumstances. But this was far from normal and ordinary. He had just done that intense staring thing as he had stripped out of his suit slowly. I was in some kind of state that was near to disbelief I think. All of that edging - all of that mind melting and now I was going to get what I had asked for. Correction what I had begged for. At least it seemed that was what I was going to get. That was the thing, nothing was ever as it seemed. It was like the moment I had sat at that table with Geena and Rob, in the club, nothing was as it seemed. And it had just got more and more so like that as the night went on and now there was this. My eyes opened wide when I saw Rob's cock. It was huge. Not that I had ever seen or had anything to compare it with. It just looked brutal. I wondered had he been hard, this hard the whole way through. It stood to reason that he had been hard back in the club when he knew what Geena was doing to me. And now that hardness, that erection, that pulsating mass of cock was dribbling from the pee hole. It seems that there was so much pressure behind that erection that it was forcing this fluid out of him.

It would be that fluid, and my own that would act as lubrication. I had to sit on his lap facing away from him. I didn't mind that. I didn't really want to see his face or be close to him like that and so facing away from him was fine. More than fine. I gasped when I felt him rub his cock head up and down my dripping lips. I was squatting over him then, one of my stiletto feet either side of his thighs. And I was lowering myself down slowly. Lowering myself down and letting him do that rubbing thing on my sex lips. It was when he did that that the size of that cock became real. It had been surreal when I saw it first but now it was in contact with my flesh it was real. I don't know how to explain the noise I

57

made when he slipped that huge cock head into me. There was a grunt that came from deep in my tummy I knew that. But there was this other sound as well. That was a wet obscene sound that in a way I was pleased that no-one else could hear. I swallowed dryly even if the sounds I made were wet ones. And then he was holding on to my hips and he was pulling me down onto him. His cock was taking my breath away. I could feel the sheer size of it stretching me and invading me at the same time. I was sure that he was going to make me bleed or something. He felt so big, so hard. But I didn't bleed. I just opened up more and more for him and I absorbed him. It was like I was so hungry that my sexuality just ate him up.

I'm not sure how to explain or describe what it felt like to have this man inside me like this. He pulled me all the way down so that I was sitting on his lap with his cock fully embedded inside me. Being penetrated like this was a relief after so much of that edging. That edging brought so many needs and wants to the surface but this cock inside me was making me feel like it had all been worth it. It was making me feel good. I think my body, as well as my mind was in a state of shock. But I was getting through that. I was coming through to the other side of that. And then when he was fucking me slowly, he was lifting me by the hips and then letting me down again. Then lifting me and letting me down again. It felt like I was sliding up and down the length of his cock and that each time I did that I was having my breath taken away. But there was another feeling that was coming through. The same feeling that happened when Geena had been edging me. That being taken to the edge - right at that moment of being on the edge when the pleasure was almost too much to bare. Like when I thought I might pass out or something.

But I didn't pass out. I could feel myself squeezing the inside of my sex around that massive cock and I found that if I did that, the feeling, that edging feeling was more and more intense. It was like I could control what I couldn't control when Geena was doing it with her fingers. This was a different edging though. This was an edging with me 'full' of that cock. And because I was full and because I was so stretched and full it was a different, intense, but different feeling. And he was guiding me - guiding me by the hips. Up and down, up and down. And then he would alter the angle of his hips so that the pressure was directed at different parts of the inside of my cunt. He was slipping in and out in and out and as he was doing that I could feel him staring at the back of my head. In a way I was grateful that he couldn't see my face but at the same time I wanted him to see my face. Not that I knew what I looked like. I hadn't felt like this before so didn't know what my face looked like or what I looked like. All I did know that I was coming closer and closer to that edge with every one of his in strokes. It was like when he was pulling me back down by the hips, he was inside me as far as he would go. I know now that he was pummelling his cock up against my cervix. I didn't know that then - back then I just thought that he had come to the end of the line.

As he was fucking me I had my hands down between my spread legs and I was doing, or attempting to do with my fingers what Geena had been doing. Except that I had decided that I wouldn't edge myself. I had decided that I would go that one step further and that I would find out first-hand what was beyond that edging feeling. I cannot describe or explain the sensations I was getting. I was receiving a two-layer pleasure - intense pleasure. The pleasure that the cock was giving me. That was a pleasure that was provided by its sheer size. I didn't know then that it was the start of my own cravings. That I would have a lot of cravings and that cock, big cock would be just one of them. I didn't know that then - how could I? The other pleasure source was my fingers and what they were doing with my clitoris. I knew about my clit. Any self-respecting teenager knows about her clit. I knew but I didn't know what it could give me. I didn't know exactly how much pleasure that it could give. I didn't know how intense the pleasure that it could give could be. I let myself be fucked by this man Rob. The man who didn't say a word. He either stared or he fucked, or he did both.

When I passed the point of return - when I passed that edge and spilled over, I was gushing juices. Or rather I was squirting them. The pressure of the pleasure behind my sex lips, and behind my clitoris was just so great that I squirted and squirted. I have to admit I was a bit afraid of what was happening to me. It was like the pleasure, that undiluted pleasure did not stop building and building even though I had gone past the edge and I didn't know where it was all going to end. Just a build and a build and then a full cry orgasm rocked right through me. And I know that Rob was offloading inside me as well, at the same time, because I could feel the pressure of that as well. Him whitewashing my inner walls and my cervix with his semen as I pulsated an orgasm that seemed to fill my entire being. I had things in my mind that at last I had been over that edge and found out what was on the other side and now I could just get on with life. That kind of filled me with a glow - like a warm glow inside of me. But I was going to find out that there was no happy ever after t accompany that glow.

I came down from what I know now was an intense, super-orgasm and I thought I would just be back into some form of normality and that I would just thank Geena and the mute Rob for the good time and they could just drop me back off in town and I would find my own way home from there. But it wasn't like that. Yes I came down from the orgasm. I came down from that but the need was still there. There was still this need in me that was itching at the very core of my sexuality. It wasn't supposed to be like this. I got the come down from the orgasm but I got that it wasn't enough as well. I could still feel myself needy. And when Rob pushed me off his cock I wanted him to be still inside me. I wanted him to fill me up again. And I wanted to play with my clit still. I didn't get it. Normal people cannot have been like this. Normal people had sex and then they got on with their lives. Why was this not happening with me? And why was I feeling guilty about this as well, on top of everything else? I felt 'gaping' from where Rob had been inside me. And I was aware of Geena, on the side-lines just watching me. She wasn't saying anything, she was just watching. She knew about my need not going away. She knew what was happening with me. I didn't know that at the time but I know it now. "You still need don't you sweetheart? You still need so much? If you're a good girl, if you are a really good girl, maybe you'll get pleasure. Maybe not."

There was something about Geena's voice that time. It was like there was something hidden inside that voice. Like a hidden meaning. And at the same time, I could feel something slipping away from me. At the time, again, I didn't know what it was. But now I know that it was like my 'freedom' slipping away from me. My control. This woman and this man had taken me to this place and they had done what they set out to do. They had put this need in me - like they had injected this need in me that couldn't be sated and couldn't be removed. And there was that thing again, that 'good girl' thing. I was feeling that I would have to be a good girl in many ways in order to receive any pleasure. In my mind that was ok - I could deal with that. But the reality was not as easy or simple to cope with. And with what I know now, being a good girl for this woman, for this couple, would prove to be in a way nightmarish. More so than I could imagine, ever. And on top of everything I had the guilt. There was guilt in droves. The need seemed to feed the guilt and the guilt seemed to feed the need. I was in a no-win situation. But then I had been in that no-win situation from the time that Geena and Bob had spotted me. In fact, I had been in a no-win situation for a lot longer than that.

Chapter 7

A little earlier

Tina, Tara's mum looked at the clock on the wall. She knew that the clubs didn't throw out until as last as 3am. But it was gone 5am now and it was getting light outside. In her mind Tara should be home now. Yes, no doubt she would be the worse for wear but she was sure that her one and only would be home by this time safe and sound. The fact was that she wasn't. She reasoned with herself that Tara was growing up, that she HAD grown up and she knew how to look after herself. It was probably that she had got talking to friends and had lost track of time. Or they had gone to their favourite bench in the park and sat down yapping and laughing. That would be it! There would be a simple explanation. Tara would come waltzing through the door any minute with that big sexy smile on her face. Yes, that was it. That was what would happen. She was kind of convinced in an unconvinced way that that would happen. Still it niggled her though.

Tina had been drinking wine - that was normal for her when she was home. But there were traces of white stuff around her upper lip and her nostrils as well. She had done a few lines of coke. She wasn't an addict. She had never been an addict but the coke had helped her through difficult times. Back in the day when she was doing things for money that she preferred never to have to think about, she did a few lines just to get her through. Maybe even she binged on it but she could always walk away from it, she was never addicted to it. She could get herself through her latest sexual indignity in the return for cash and then she could walk away from the white stuff. That was always how it had been. Some people used it recreationally, some people were addicted to it

63

and Tina was somewhere in between. She was in a group of her own. But then she always had been. If she had ever been asked about the cocaine thing she would have said that the white stuff was her friend. Like a best friend that got her through things. That didn't explain why she had to have it this night though. There was no reason for it. Ok, ok, Tara was late home. In actual fact she wasn't late at all. She didn't have to be at home at a certain time. Those days were long gone. And besides, Tina and the way she had come through life hardly lent itself to her laying rules and regulations on Tara. But still, she had hit the wine early - but she always did that. And then about 2am for some reason she had snorted the line of coke. And then another.

She wouldn't be able to put her finger on it but Tina was feeling uneasy inside herself and she didn't know why. It was like there was this little nagging at a set of nerves that were so deeply buried in her femininity that she hadn't known they even were there. Actually, it wasn't even nagging, it was a full-on grating of her nerves. She felt uneasy about something and she didn't know what, or why. Like she was agitated or anxious - or both. And on top of that Tara wasn't home yet. Tina, above all others would know about the dangers out there. Tina had been a woman of the night and she had known, still knew, all about the weirdos and out and out sick fucks there were out there. Maybe it was because she was so in the know that she had this uneasy feeling. Maybe it would have been better if she didn't have the insight that she had into 'that' side of life. But the fact was that she did. She did know about the lower levels of life that existed in a big city. She cut up another line of coke with a credit card on the glass coffee table and she got down on her knees to snort it through a rolled up twenty. Then she tossed her head back whilst the white stuff did its job. She fucking hated this feeling she was getting. And the coke wasn't doing so much to alleviate it at all. If anything, it was enhancing and emphasising the unease.

Usually a line or two and she was fine. Not this time. She got the buzz, but she also got the cut through of that agitated feeling she had been suffering. She considered doing another line but decided against that. She didn't want to tip into addiction. That was easy enough to do, god knows she had seen it often enough. She looked at the clock again, 5.30am. She tilted her head back against the seat of the sofa and she was remembering. She was remembering things from back in the day. She didn't want to go there but it was like she couldn't help herself. For the time being she was having her mind taken off Tara and that fact that she wasn't home yet. Which was the lesser of two evils? Thinking about the good old days - that was a laugh - the good old days. Or thinking about the myriad of things that could have happened to Tara? No, she couldn't go there. She had to sink into the memories of her past. The things she used to do to make ends meet. She wished she didn't have to do it, but she did. It would set her off again - she knew it would. But better that she killed some more time this way, than think of the worse until Tara came home.

The Past

Tina couldn't have been more than eighteen. A pretty white English girl. The Muslims and the Pakistanis loved them. It was just a thing they had. A thing - like the way they treated all girls and women, but in particular white English women. They thought they were the lowest of the low and treated them as such. The problem with the culture was that they took it to this country from their own country. They thought they could apply the same rules that they did at home. The same values, the same 'ways'. And because they came here and didn't mingle with society, in general that is, because they didn't become part of our society they built their own 'townships' in inner cities and so they only ever had their own rules to live by. Of course, not limited to inner cities any more, the spread was apparent, ever apparent. White English girls of all ages had to be careful - beyond careful in fact, not to be lured in, because once they were in, they were in. They wouldn't be able to saunter out like they sauntered in. Once they were in they were in.

But other white English girls had to be careful as well. Ones that had fallen into the grips of street life and prostitution. Tina fell into that group. Already vulnerable and already giving herself in return for the most basic level of income. Of course, it didn't help if a pimp was taking the majority of the proceeds. It didn't help that a pimp had latched on the someone like Tina and then worked on her. The odd bottle of wine or spirits. The odd line of cheap coke. Working to bring her into the system. Grooming her, preparing her. That was all it was. Bringing her into the system. And then of course once she was there it was easy to keep her there. It was easy to farm her out to the ones that paid the most money. Tina gratifying one or more of the Asian groups was common. She was used to it. But because she was used to it, didn't mean that she liked it. It didn't mean that she could simply grin and bear it. It didn't mean that because she was used to it, she didn't get the nightmares or the flashbacks. She did get those flashback and nightmares and this was proof of that.

She never saw any money changing hands, ever. Rather she would just be taken to one of the communities and she would be left there. It was never a quick job, in and then out. It was always like a job-lot. The pimp would be paid for the day, or the night, or both. And then Tina would just have to turn up and be her pretty self. Just be that white English girl that the group wanted. She would always remember the first time. Just about old enough and dropped off to this seedy place. This terrible place. It stunk of illegal substances and mingled with that was a strong stench of urine. It was called an 'apartment'. It wasn't an apartment, it was a shit hole. Tina would always remember it as a shit hole. She had taken the time to make herself up and look nice and she had no idea that it was that that these people wanted to ruin the look of. They wanted to ruin her but they wanted to ruin how she looked the most. Four, five, six even seven men all waiting for her in this stench of a place. The walls dirty, the floors filthy. The furniture old and reeking of cigarettes and alcohol.

"On your knees bitch. You can suck us all one at a time until we decide what the real fun will be about." Tina had been petrified. Just those words, on your knees bitch. It wasn't the words but the way they were said. There was just no respect in there at all. They had paid for her and as far as they were concerned her ass belonged to them for that time. There was no doubt that if Tina hadn't been controlled by a pimp, they would have taken possession of her full time and full stop. In a way it was good that Tina had the pimp to protect her. But this was early days, very early days. These were the days before Tina would make the break out to do things on her own. And these were the days long, long before Tara came along. This was Tina learning from the bottom rung of the ladder. Learning the basics as it were.

There would be other things that Tina would remember from her past years. In lots of ways worse things than this. But this first time with the Asians and with the Muslims, this is what she would always remember. If she had ever been asked to say what it was like to feel one of those cocks sliding into her mouth, what it was like to 'taste' one of those cocks, she would never be able to. That was mainly because that night there were seven or eight cocks she had to suck. Not two of them the same. Cocks that she had to suck to completion. Brown cocks in her mouth one after the other and unprotected. She had remembered her pimp's words, "make sure they're happy. Its good money and it makes me happy." It was all he said and from that she got that she would have to do anything and everything that was required of her for these obscene men. And they were obscene men. No six packs and handsome chaps here. Smelly obese and mostly older men who were well entrenched in their own customs and culture. Tina had hated those cocks in her mouth. It wasn't so bad once she had washed the cock in question off with her own saliva. Once she had washed its taste off and her saliva coated it then it wasn't too bad. The sucking of the cocks one at a time wasn't too bad it was having them men look down on her the way they did. It was the way they spoke and treated her as she was pleasuring them that almost made her vomit.

Of course it could have been the copious amounts of semen that she tasted and swallowed that almost made her vomit. That could have been it. But she had sucked cocks before this time. It was just the first time she was in this environment, this toxic, stinking environment. That is what made her want to wretch. But she couldn't do that. She couldn't wretch and vomit. That would be a failure and it would be reported as such back to her pimp. She hadn't let her pimp down this far but she was pretty sure as to what would happen if she did let him down. She had seen the state of other girls who had let him down and she didn't want to end up like that. So, she had to work her mouth through that urge to puke.

She had to work through it any way she could. And the thing with Tina was that she was always 'talented' with her mouth. Even from that early age she was good at pleasuring cocks orally. It was like it was a talent that she had been born with. Like one that she hadn't needed to learn. Or one that had come naturally to her. And she had just 'got' what the addition of some red lipstick did. She kind of knew it was just decoration for her mouth when the cocks slid in one after the other. There had never been any of this feminist stuff with Tina. It was like she had always known her place. Like she had always known what rung of the food ladder she was on. And she simply accepted that. She accepted it until that is she broke away to do it her way. It would be different then, but for now, for this pimp and for these Asians and Muslims she had to do it their way. She had to be what they wanted her to be. She had to be everything they wanted her to be.

Sucking those cocks 'lovingly' and 'dutifully' that night was only part of the story - a very small part of the story. The process of sucking seven or eight cocks was a long one and so by the time she had sucked the last one dry of its semen, the first guys were ready for more action. It was more or less non-stop for Tina that night. A full on debauched session for her to endure. She was little more than a cum-dump for these men. The taste of stale semen would be in her mouth if not hours then days after the event. But it would be the memories of her crawling round on that floor from man to man - making him hard and finishing him off. And then her crawling round and spreading her knees wide so they could enter her from behind.

It was just the whole 'filth' of what she was involved in that night that would never leave her. It was like one of those nightmarish, dystopian scenes in which the Muslims had taken over the world. And in amongst this was this white English prostitute gratifying these disgusting men. And even when they had sated themselves - even when they couldn't repeat anymore there would be the abuse to come. One man making Tina stay on her hands and knees in front of him on the floor, making her spread her legs wide and then making her stay just like that as he continually toe poked her sex. Him sliding his big horrible toe inside her and then him making her suck it clean. Bearing in mind that she had had a lot of deposits of semen up inside her by this time she was sucking this mixed semen off a brown person's big toe. And she had to do it like she liked it. She had to do it liked she 'loved' doing it. Like she was grateful for being allowed to do it.

And then there was the one who simply made her kneel up in front of him and hold her hands behind her head as he slapped and spat on her breasts and in her face. "White trash girl. You belong to us now." That had mortified her to hear that. It made her think that the pimp had sold her to them and that she actually belonged to them. But that couldn't be right. Whatever it simply added to her absolute nightmare of a situation. Holding her hands behind her head and keeping them there as this man mauled her breasts, twisted her nipples and then slapped the larger globes of mammary flesh. Each slap made her breasts ripple and dance. And then this man, this same man pinching the nipples between his thumbs and forefingers and then lifting the breasts up by her nipples, suspending them. That hurt her. She had had to bite down on her bottom lip when he did that. The slaps weren't so bad, they just stung. But the pinch of the nipples and the lift of the breasts, that hurt that did. Maybe more than one to two tears rolled down her heavily made up cheeks at that time.

That was what these men did. They ruined her look. The look that had needed to be perfect at the start but which the pimp knew would be ruined within a relatively short space of time. Tina had had to be beyond perfect to begin with. Something that she was more than capable of doing even at her very young age. And now this. There was this one fat Asian man, middle aged who insisted that she get across his lap so that he could give some attention to her lily-white buttocks. Maybe she thought she would be spanked. She had been spanked before, funnily enough by non-Muslims. But no, it wasn't a spanking that he gave her. It was a strapping with his own heavy leather belt. And he had held her vice like, in a tight grip, as he had laid on that belt. "This is what white trash, 'our' white trash gets, you slut." And the thing was that she hadn't known whether she could cry or not. She wanted to cry. That belting hurt her a lot and she could feel the welts rise even as he was putting more on. But she thought if she cried that might be wrong, and that it wasn't what these awful men wanted. But if she didn't cry then maybe he would just keep laying on that belt until she did, or until something else gave. It was no win for Tina whichever way it went.

Memories of that night were always, would always be vivid in Tina's mind. It was just the way it was. There were other non-pleasant memories - a lot of them, even from after she broke out alone. Even from the nights when she used to go out and leave Tara. Those nights that she would sneak in in the small hours. She was always grateful that Tara was nearly always fast asleep when she came home those nights because of some of the states that she was in. She wouldn't have wanted Tara to see her like that. She wouldn't have been able to live with herself if Tara had even glimpsed her like that in the slightest amount. She was always pleased with herself how come the morning she was this bright and breezy mother again. That was when she could push the memories of what she had done the night before to the back of her mind. That was when she could switch off from that other person that she was. That hooker that went out and gratified paying customers sexually. That was when she could become a mother again.

Chapter 8

Now

Tina had been in that slumber for some time. Sitting on the floor in the deep pile carpet, up against the sofa, her head back and lolling side to side as she remembered that first Muslim encounter. The cocaine had softened the memories a little bit. The white stuff had blurred the hard edges just a tiny bit. But they were still nightmarish scenes. She opened her eyes and was startled. Like at first she couldn't remember where she was or why she was there. It was only very slowly, very gradually that realisation came to her. It was the first thing she remembered, where she was. Then her eyes opened wide and she was even more startled. Those eyes flicked to the wall clock, it was past 7am. Then she remembered Tara wasn't home. The last time she had looked at the clock it was 5.30am. Maybe her one and only had come in, found her asleep and gone to bed deciding not to wake her mum.

But that would have been unlike Tara. Tina knew whenever Tara got home, no matter what time it was, she would be buzzing and would want to talk. It was always the way it was. But Tina managed to get to her feet. Her legs felt weak, and more than a little wobbly. But she made it upstairs and she swung open Tara's bedroom door. Her bed hadn't been slept in. Tina's head was banging. That would have been a mixture of the wine effect and the cocaine effect. The come down. Now she had that drink and drugs cocktail mix and the fact that Tara wasn't home yet to contend with. She checked her cell phone. She had always told Tara to make sure she called, or make sure she sent her a text message if she was going to be late, or if she was going to be doing something out of the ordinary, or if she was in any sort of trouble. There had been no missed calls and no messages received. She did the first thing that came into her head and she pressed to call Tara. But that was odd, Tara's number went straight to voicemail. Her cell phone never, but never went straight to voice! Now Tina was seriously getting worried. The night before, she had had a niggle, like a little agitation going on, but now there was something for her to worry about. It was daylight outside and not even a text message from her one and only. That had never happened before, ever!

The drink and the cocaine in her blood stream were an added agitation to the already established concern for her girl. Just out of curiosity she held a hand up and it was shaking. That could have been down to any of the ingredients within her. The anxiety, the wine, the coke. And a mixture of them all. She reached for her cigarettes. Just for a split second she had considered another line of coke. But she discounted that. She needed a clear head. She needed to think and she wouldn't be able to do that if her head was buzzing from a snort of coke. She lit a cigarette, dragged and then inhaled deeply. She got the nicotine hit and that calmed her a little bit more. She tried to think of what to do. At first she couldn't think and that was just it - she couldn't think. Then she remembered, Tara had gone out with Candice amongst others. They had been friends for a long time. She considered calling her but it was too early in the morning to do that. Then she decided, no it wasn't. Tara wasn't home and she didn't have a fucking clue where she was, or who she was with. And on top of that she was approaching blind panic mode. She thumbed through the phone book in her own phone and found Candice's number.

Unlike Tara's phone, Candice's didn't go to voice mail. Instead it rang and rang. Tina was almost going to give up and hang up but then the weary, tired voice of

Candice came through the speaker. "Hi Tina, what's up?" Tina had always had this rule where Tara's friends could call her by her first name. She couldn't be doing with all the polite politically correct shit. "Hi Candice, I was just wondering is Tara with you - she didn't come home last night and to be honest I'm more than a little worried." Tina voice was shaky, she could feel that for herself. God only knew what it sounded like to Candice. There was this moment, or few moments of silence where Candice didn't answer. But then she cut in, "We left her talking to this couple in the club but she was ok. We made sure she was ok before we left. Seriously, maybe she just went back to theirs for a night cap or something. I'm sure she's fine. Did you try to call her?" And there was this silence again. "Yeah I did but it went straight to voice." Another silence. Tina was thinking that ok, maybe Tara was on some kind of adventure. A couple in a night club. It stood to reason. Tina didn't like to think of Tara growing up in that way. But she was of that age now. Her hormones were in all likelihood raging and she would inevitably have adventures. Tina preferred that word, 'adventures'. Of course, she knew what she meant!

But now there was the question of not wanting to disturb Tara if this was the case. Besides, Tina's mind was a little more at ease now that she knew there was this older couple in the mix there somewhere. For some reason she thought that it was ok that there was this strange couple in the mix. Maybe she was thinking that at least her one and only hadn't gone off in a car full of Asians, Muslims or blacks. That would have been the ultimate horror nightmare scenario. If Candice had told her that Tara had got into a car with a load of those types. But now she was willing to give her a little longer. Given the fact that Candice had seen this couple and that she had said that she was ok. She would give her a little longer. "Look Candice, its ok. I just wanted to know if you knew anything. I'll give her a bit longer and try her number again. Thanks sweetheart." And there was this little click as she hung up. She wouldn't have known that Candice was looking at her phone and a little worried herself now. Wondering if she had made the right choice to leave her friend in that club like that. But then she had been all the worse for wear herself and so. They were all big girls now after all. The big wide world out there and all that.

Tina decided, shower and tidy up. Do herself up a bit for when Tara got back. That was a good idea. She stripped off and stood in her full-length dressing mirror running her fingers down over her breasts. For a woman who had seen life, both in years and the nasty side, she looked very, very good. It had always been commented about how her and Tara look more like sisters than mother and daughter. But despite the wine and the coke, Tina looked after herself. She was in good shape. She had this tall, curvy, almost Amazonian body that defied her years and her lifestyle. That was one of the things she was always grateful for - that she still looked good and she did. She turned one way in the mirror and then the other. She looked at her bottom. She did a little smile that she always did when she looked at herself in the mirror. But the fact was that smile wasn't quite the same. She still had this nagging, grating feeling about Tara. That wouldn't leave her. Maybe it was the fact that just because she now had a little insight into what Tara had been up to the night before, she still didn't know where she was, what she was doing or who she was with.

The hot water running over her head and face and down over her huge breasts was like a godsend. She held her head back in the shower and let her dirty blonde hair take the hit as well as her face and neck. She stood there for ages. Just stood there and let this hot steaming water cascade over her face. Her nostrils flared a little bit as she played her fingers over her nipples. She did both nipples at the same time and they seemed to spring to life immediately. Her fleshy wet tongue touched the corner of her mouth as her hands travelled down. She found her smooth, hairless, plump sex lips and she just ever so lightly dragged one finger between them. Her lips pursed and she blew out a silent 'ohhhh'. She was still alive down there - she hadn't lost it. She often thought it was weird after all that she had been through, how come she didn't just feel nothing down there. She would have understood it if her body had reacted like that. If after years of abuse and sexual servitude, that it all had just given up on her and let her be sexless for the rest of her life. But it hadn't done that. She had been amazed, stunned even to realise that she was even more sexual now than she had been during those bad years. It was like when she had left it all behind she had come really and totally to life.

She washed her hair. That was always a mission. Her hair was thick mane of soft curls. Dirty blonde in that it wasn't pure blonde or platinum blonde. Ditty blonde and not out of a bottle, she liked that and always smiled when it came to her mind. She washed her body as well. She stayed in that shower longer than it would take anyone normally to simply shower. But that was the after effects of the night before. And besides with that hot water cascading over her like that, it helped her think. It helped her try to put things in perspective. Tara was in her mind though and she could not get away from that. She just couldn't. What if this couple weren't good at all? That question played and then replayed time after time. Each time she dismissed it though as though to tell herself that the odds of her one and only being picked up by a dodgy couple were pretty slim. A dodgy man. A dodgy group of men - fair enough. But a dodgy couple? The chances of that happening were more than next to nil. In a strange way that made Tina chill a little bit. She would get this shower out of the way and she would get herself dressed up, made up and in the hours it would take her to do that, something would happen. Tara would come home or she would call, or she would get a text message. Yes, that would be it - something would happen.

Except it didn't. Two hours later Tina looked more like a hooker than she had looked when she WAS a hooker, except now she did it with a bit of style and class. She had thought, with it being the weekend that she would wait till Tara got back and they would go out and do lunch - spend the afternoon shopping. Do the girlie thing together even if they were mother and daughter. They did that sometimes. Go out for lunch, which would be a long liquid lunch, then go shopping and then go to dinner all in one hit. And Tina had the feeling that was what she wanted to do today. But it didn't work out like that either. If anything - as she looked at her watch, it was gone ten and she was getting a little bit angry. Angry on one hand and worried on the other. She was sure, as sure as she could be that Tara would call her and let her know she was ok. Yes maybe, just maybe she had lost track of time but she was sure that at some point Tara would snap out of it and think, 'shit I have to call mum'. But then on the other hand there was the fact that if she was in trouble, she wouldn't be able to call. She tried her cell phone again. Nothing - straight to voice.

Tina had this rule - she never opened the wine until after mid-day. She had had this rule ever since she could remember. She even knew about this rule now, but it didn't matter. She needed a drink. She needed to feel the alcohol bite at the back of her throat and she needed to get that little bit of a light-headed feeling going again.

She could cope better that way. And besides, she didn't know how this day was going to pan out. She already wasn't liking the feel of it. She already had that nagging feeling back except now it had moved to the pit of her stomach. She opened a bottle of Pinot Noir - something light for her to start the day. The trouble was that she didn't know what to do next. She was dressed in a thin almost transparent summer dress. This year was the first that she had ever gone hose free on her legs. That was only because the fake tan fad had hit her hard. But she looked good.

The makeup was a little bit heavy - a little bit over the top but that was ok. She always did it that way. She always used to say what the point in doing your makeup to make it look like you're not wearing any. How fucking pointless is that? Her hair always looked lush after it had been washed and blow dried. She always left it natural - never spent hours styling it. Tina was a bit like that - she didn't need to style herself really. She had this natural style that kind of oozed from her. It was like the older she got, the more all the bits seemed to fall into place for her. She was a thoroughly stunning woman. But also a worried one.

By mid-day she was considering calling the police. She was thinking that there wasn't much else that she could do. She needed to know where her little girl was. And by this time, she was convinced that there was something wrong. More than convinced. Her cell phone rang out of the blue. She looked at the touch screen. It was Tara's number. She snatched up the phone and pressed to answer the call. "Tara, where the fuck are you? I've been worried out of my head. Why didn't you call, or send me a text? Where are you, I'll come and get you?" Tina hadn't waited for Tara to say anything. She had just blurted it all out and then stopped. The thing was that she had this tingly feeling down the core of her spine for some reason and she didn't know what that reason was until she was answered. "Tara is safe. She's with us Tina. I wouldn't have bothered to call you, but then I thought you might do something stupid. So - you just sit tight, don't do anything, don't say anything to anyone, do NOT call the authorities, just sit tight until you hear from me again. Just have a few glasses of wine, I know you like your wine. Do a line or two. Just relax Tina. If you do anything that I have told you not to do...." And the voice, the female voice didn't finish that sentence. She left it hanging as though she didn't need to elaborate further. Then there was this click and the phone went dead.

Tina was in shock. This changed everything - absolutely everything. That voice, that woman - it was like she knew Tina or something. And now there was no doubt that Tara was in some kind of trouble. What was she supposed to do? The called been hung up. Everything was fucked up now. Now she had to really think on her feet. But she didn't know what she was supposed to do. She had been told by this 'voice' just to sit tight and do nothing. Just chill, do some more wine and maybe do some coke. Who the fuck was that woman? All of this was going round and round in Tina's mind. At one point she decided the only thing she could do was to call the police. She got her phone and almost thumbed the 'emergency call' button on the touch screen. But then she stopped. She couldn't do it. If she did that, that woman, the one that had just called her would know and then god only knows what would happen to Tara. She topped her wine up. Her mind was in a whirl. Then she went to her stash of coke. She knew it would be wrong to start snorting lines now but it was like that escape was calling her. Like her mind was so fucked up that it would be completely justified for her to do a line or two. She didn't have much left. She would have to call her dealer to drop off a fresh stash.

She made that call to the dealer but did what she had left of the last lot. If anything, she OD'd on the last of that but she threw her head back and got lost in the buzz before it died down again. When she brought her head back down again she reached for the Pinot and took a big gulp. Then she tried to think. She had to try to think through the haze again. The haze of the alcohol and the coke. She had to at least try to think logically but she couldn't. There was just too much going through her mind. There was just too much happening inside her head and trying to put it all into logical thoughts wasn't happening. Then she did the maths herself. She had been told to sit tight. She had been told to chill and do nothing. Then surely that was she had to do? Was that woman a woman from her past? Did she know her? It sure sounded as though the woman knew her. And in her mind there was this familiarity there. But again, it was something that she couldn't put her finger on. Or maybe it was just the guilt from her past wreaking havoc on her psyche.

There was this bead, this thread of absolute panic going through Tina but there was nothing that she could do about it. That was the thing - there was absolutely nothing that she could do about it. So, she began to pace the room. If anything, Tina was good on her high heels - she always had been and just because she was in panic mode, didn't mean her hips didn't sway right, or her tits didn't roll as she strutted on those heels. She paced the room and she drank wine. Occasionally she would light a cigarette and smoke it heavily. Even more occasionally she would get down to the glass coffee table and do a line of coke. If she had been asked what got her through the most, the coke, the alcohol or the cigarettes. She would say all of them. That was a fact. Then she began to feel herself crying. She was in despair and there was no way out of it. Now all she could do was wait. But she didn't even know how long she would have to wait for. She sat on the floor again, in that deep pile carpet and she leaned back against the sofa. For just a few seconds there was nothing except the sound of her rapid breathing. But then she sobbed and she didn't stop sobbing. She simply sobbed her heart out.

Chapter 9

Earlier that same night

I don't know why but I knew that Geena was in the process of turning my cell phone off. She had been thumbing through it and then she was turning it off. I knew as well that if I didn't call mum, she would eventually call me. If she couldn't get hold of me she would worry. I knew that as well. But now, Geena was looking right at me as my phone was shut down and there was this slight smile on her face as she did that. Then she tossed the phone into her bag. I'm not sure that I was grasping the whole picture or what it meant. Like I don't think I was grasping the enormity of what was happening. It had gone from a night out, and a chance meeting with these people, to them holding me here now. And to me being in some kind of sexual mire. The trouble was that I couldn't think straight because of that need that was still inside me. That sexual need and the desperation to orgasm again. That was what I needed the most - another of those orgasms. I would literally kill for another of those 'things' again. I felt that I needed one badly and anything else, even mum worrying about me, even me being held here like this, even me not knowing where this little adventure was going to end, just didn't matter. It just wasn't important. Feeling that sensation though, down there - now that was at the top of my list. It was at the very top of my list.

"If you are a good girl, I won't hurt you too much." Rob wasn't a mute after all and he shocked me when he did speak those first words. He hadn't said a word all night. Not in the club, not in the car back to this house. And he hadn't even said a word when he was buried balls deep in me, rutting me like a bull. But now - now that he had deposited his semen inside of me, now that that was over and done with he decides to come out with that. I didn't know what was the matter with me, I just didn't. I had wanted penetration so badly I would have done anything. Indeed, what I had done was let a complete stranger be inside me unprotected and he had gone all the way. I thought that would be enough. I thought that I wouldn't have wanted any more - especially when I saw the size of that cock. Especially when I saw the thickness of it. There was no way that I would want more after that, except I did. The need inside me didn't leave me. It didn't even lessen. If anything, the need and the 'urge' only increased. It only got more so. It was like something that was just working on me. Like something that was all I could think about.

"I'll be a good girl, I promise I'll be a good girl." And the thing was that I meant it. I truly meant it that I would be a good girl for this man. Even though I didn't even know what being a good girl for him meant. He had already fucked me. He had already impaled me on that massive, massive cock. And he had already spent himself up inside me so I didn't know how much more of a good girl I could be. Or I didn't know how else I could be a good girl. "Suck me nice a clean. Suck me like you mean it and suck me clean. Show me what a good girl you can be." I guess that was part of the answer to my question. His cock was coated with his own semen dregs. But it was also coated with 'me'. I should have been disgusted by what he was telling me to do. But the fact was that the need, the arousal in me was still so great that I didn't care. It was like because what he was telling me to do was so sexually related, it was so sexual, that it kind of tickled that arousal in me. I actually WANTED to have that cock in my mouth. I actually wanted to taste it, and clean it. It was as though my fucked up rewired sexuality felt that it would go some way to gratification if I did that obscene thing. I was

84

drooling, literally at the thought of cleaning that cock with my mouth and with my lips and with my tongue.

He slapped that cock around my face first. Just letting me know it was there for me to clean. Those cock slaps were heavy around my cheeks. Those slaps making me realise the sheer size and volume of the cock. Then there was the actual act of getting that cock into my mouth. It was 'huge'. And close up it was even more huge. It wasn't rigid hard but it wasn't flaccid either. But I sank my mouth over it like I was so hungry. That was because I WAS so hungry. I needed to taste it and I needed to taste 'me'. My mouth made obscene noises as it slipped over the enormous bell end and I could feel the immediate 'ache' with how wide my jaws had to open in order to get that bell into my mouth. I sucked that dick head clean first. Polishing the purple bell with my lips and tongue and making sure that I 'tasted' everything that came off it. And then I cleaned the shaft. That thick, vein ridden shaft. There wasn't the hardness there now. It was more like a flaccid firmness that I had to clean. But there was plenty of meat. "Don't touch yourself. Don't cum. Don't you DARE cum."

That had been Geena speaking from the side-lines. I could have cried but didn't. I was hoping I could have touched myself, slipped some fingers into myself and played with my clitoris as I cleaned that cock. That would have gratified me. But she had stopped that now. Now I had to suck all sloppy and dirty and I wasn't allowed to touch myself or cum at all. In all honesty I didn't know if I would be able to stop myself cumming - even though I wasn't touching I could feel that pressure and pleasure build behind my saturated swollen clitoris the same as if I was touching. Or the same as if I was being touched by someone else. In a way I wished I hadn't felt that cock up inside me because then I wouldn't be so needy now. But that I had felt it made me even more drooling for it. I had to get through this I really did.

It was hard, so hard for me to not touch myself. It was even harder for me not to cum. I had to imagine that I was being edged again. I had to imagine that I was being edged by someone else and that I had no control. That was the only way that I could do it. But that only made me more horny doing it like that. As I cleaned that cock I was becoming more and more needy of that taste. I didn't know what this couple were doing to me, how could I? In my mind I was edging myself and holding back. Edging and holding back. It was the only way that I could do it - it was the only way that I could stop myself from cumming. That just got harder and harder. It came to the point that I almost said, 'fuck it' and let myself cum anyway. But inside my mind I was still thinking about being that good girl. I sucked and cleaned that cock like my life depended on it. There would be a question, that if my life did actually depend on it, would I be doing it more for that, or for the sheer pleasure the sheer need that I had to feel that intense pleasure? I twirled my tongue around Rob's pee hole. Like I needed to get it all out of that - nothing could be left. I sucked the bell hard and firmly. I think I spent more time with that bell in my mouth just because it was such a beautiful thing. It felt all smooth and big in my mouth and it tasted, well the taste simply fed my need more and more.

"I'm going to put these up inside you. And you need to hold them inside you until I tell you otherwise. You'll need to squeeze them to keep them inside you. You'll need to squeeze real tight." Geena had come around to the front of me and she was holding a set of bead like things, all connected on a string. Like a string of beads except there was a gap between each of them. Each of the beads, like stainless steel beads were identical in size. About two inches in diameter, and shiny and smooth. I looked at this string of beads wrapped over her hands. She was holding them up for me to see. I was trying to compute what she had just said. She was going to put these things inside me. Inside my sex? Oh my! Was that what she meant? I didn't know. That would mean 'attention' to me down there. That was ok, I needed and wanted attention down there badly. I tried to imagine how I would manage with these things being slid up inside me. I tried to wonder if an orgasm would force itself on me and whether or not I would be able to stop it. I wondered if imagining that I was edging would be enough to stop the flow of a real orgasm with those things being slipped up inside me one at a time. All smooth and big. Just stretching my lips a little bit and then 'popping' inside of me. The more I thought about it the more I was doubtful that I would be able to cope with not cumming. And yet at the same time, the more I thought about it the more I wanted it. My mind was doing cartwheels trying to imagine and trying to 'feel' those beads being put up inside me.

But in the event I had it wrong. I had it all wrong. The beads were for my other place. My other hole. My bottom! I was so shocked when I found out that that was what Geena meant when she said that this string of stainless steel beads or balls would be put up inside me. She meant that she was going to feed and push them one at a time inside my bottom. When I realised that I was shocked. So shocked! I tried to get my head around it but was finding that hard. It was as though she had made her announcement and then knew that I would assume that those beads were going to be slipped up inside the warm wet swamp that was my sexuality. And it was like she wasn't in a rush to correct me. She wasn't in rush to put me right. It was like she was letting my mind wander and letting my mind make up these things. It was like she was letting the need and the greed in me to consume me before she put it right. "They're for your ass Tara. One at a time I am going to push them up inside you and you are going to squeeze them so so tight, until I tell you otherwise."

And then again I was processing her words and trying to imagine. Unfortunately, what I couldn't imagine was what the effect of having those beads slipped inside me, and then me squeezing on them would have. If there was a time when my mind had been truly blown during this time then this was it. And Geena dipped each of those beads into my pussy juice first. She turned them and twisted them in the swamp that was my sex. And that in itself was pure torment. The friction of the sliding beads, and then that same bead being slipped down between my ass cheeks. Geena was so good at locating my bottom. Just pushing against my bud softly, making sure she was in the right place and then pushing a little harder until my ass dilated. I could feel it dilate and I sucked in air. "That's a good girl. You just make sure you don't cum." There was that instruction again. I didn't think for one minute that the act of slipping these beads up inside me would make me want to cum. Or would bring me to that point of orgasm that I couldn't pull back from. But I was wrong.

I was wrong on so many levels. I was so shocked at the sensations as that first bead was pushed in that I cried out. I was even more shocked that my anus went into like a spasm and gripped the bead hard inside me. There had been that 'popping' as Geena had pushed it past the tightness of my hole first. But the way my rear sucked it in and then squeezed on it as though it was eating it, or chewing it. And all of those little chews and squeezes were feeding the sexual muscles in and around my vagina. I could feel myself breathing heavily. Very heavily. Part of that was because I knew that these sensations would become like those orgasmic ones. I was beginning to learn that it was all connected down there. And that I couldn't avoid those urges in me to cum and cum. And then Geena pushed in the second bead and I sucked in air again. She pushed this one in slowly and she didn't let it go straight away. She didn't let my ass suck it inside of me, she held it half submerged in my anus hole and she turned it. She turned it one way and then the other and I could feel my breath quickening. And as well as that I could feel my ass trying to squeeze on the ball. That squeezing was giving resistance to the turning and twisting that Geena was applying. It was like she was testing the resistance of my ass. Like she was testing the strength of my squeezes.

The thing was that I didn't want to squeeze. If I squeezed I got that feeling that I wanted to cum. And I knew I wanted to cum because I could feel all of that pressure behind my clitoris again. It was pressure but it was beautiful pressure. That is the only word that I can think of, 'beautiful'. Every time Geena slipped a bead into me using my own juices as lubrication, there was this 'sucking' sound as my ass ate the bead. Two beads, three, four, five. It got to a point that I felt full of these beads. That my rear end was full of them. At first, I tried to concentrate on not squeezing them and I did have a little bit of success with that. But the more beads that went inside me and the longer that I had to hold them for meant that I squeezed in a natural like fashion.

That is, I couldn't help myself. I guess it was a mixture of a natural thing for me to squeeze, and then the shot of absolute pleasure that I got because I squeezed like that. Whatever it was like my torment was quadrupling in my mind and in my body. Eventually I could feel my muscles in permeant state of squeeze and release, squeeze and release. It was like an involuntary masturbation that I didn't want. Oh, I wanted it but I didn't as well because I knew that with ease I could have made myself cum with these beads up inside me and with these beads enforcing the squeezing actions that my inner body, my private bits were carrying out.

"You just relax. Relax and squeeze, relax and squeeze." It was the first time that I had thought of Geena as a bitch. There were plenty of things that she could have been labelled a bitch for but this was the one. I was on a recliner and she had told me "Just lay back, open your legs nice and wide for me. Lift your knees a little bit." And she had put a pillow in the small of my back which thrust me out at the hips. And she had come to the foot of the recliner and got down on the floor between my legs. She was holding a glass of wine. Here I was in the sexual mire and in the process of having my head fucked to kingdom come. And there she was coolly calmly telling me what to do and sipping wine. I knew she knew what I was going through. She didn't say as much but it was just the way she was acting, the way she 'was'. Like her demeanour and her facial expressions said it all. She knew the torment that I was going through. And even if she didn't she might have guessed what it would to do me when she used her finger nail and just traced the outline of my sex lips. Then I was squeezing and squeezing. And there was drool coming from my mouth as well. It was just the way she was watching me. She wasn't comforting me or telling me it would be ok. She was just using her finger like that and at the same time knowing what was going on with me squeezing those beads. Those squeezes of the beads sending pleasure pulses to meet those that her finger nail was producing. She was being a bitch. An out and out bitch and I knew that. Probably so did she know as well.

She could have said something but she didn't. She sipped her wine. And as she did that she kept her finger depressed on my pulsating clitoris. She didn't need to tell me again not to cum. I got that, I knew that I couldn't cum. But what I didn't know was how long I would be able to hold off for. Rob had gone now - it was just me and Geena. And it was like she was upping some kind of anti. It was like she had done the playing around. Like she had done what she had to do to get me to this point - and now she was getting ready to up her gears. In her not saying anything, she was saying everything, if this makes sense. I could feel myself squeezing and I could feel myself approaching that orgasm again. I thought the beads inside me would drive me mad in that I would want them out of me.

But that wasn't the case at all. It just wasn't. They helped me get those shots of pleasure and they helped that build up behind my clitoris. But at the same time, they were the root cause for me having to suck back my own drool time after time. And all Geena could do was watch me. She didn't even smile. She just watched. And she moved her finger at will around my sexuality. I was aware that with each squeeze of those beads inside me that I was oozing more and more vagina drizzle. In my mind that is what I called it, vagina drizzle. Then I became aware of the wet sounds of despair that were escaping from my lips. They must have been happening for some time before I realised that they were there because from time to time Geena's expressions changed. As though she was hearing something that I wasn't - not at first anyway. Like she was taking it all in. Like she was drinking me in. Drinking in me and my despair.

Chapter 10

I was sure by now that it was despair that I was feeling. Despair that I was experiencing. And that I was losing my grip on reality. It couldn't have been anything else. It really couldn't have been. I wanted to explain to myself more than anything why I couldn't cum but I couldn't. If I couldn't explain it to myself then how would I be able to explain it to someone else? There was nothing physically stopping me from spilling into orgasm. But it was like there was this mental block there. Like as though because Geena had told me not to cum, that I just couldn't. That should have been enough of an explanation but it wasn't. There must have been enough of the logical self left in me that was trying to tell me that I didn't have to do what this woman was telling me to do. But in all honesty, that was sinking away from me more and more as a notion with every passing second.

It would have been easy for me, or for anyone who wasn't in this high state of arousal and need to have walked away. But I couldn't do that. I was lying back, my legs spread open, and this woman way simply 'playing' with me. She was simply toying with me and I was buying into it. I was buying into the fact, her fact, that I was not allowed, I was not permitted to cum. Nothing else made sense. Nothing else came anywhere close to convincing me that I didn't have to do what I was told. In the end it stood to reason that if she said, 'no orgasm' then that was the way it was. There was nothing to question. It was just the way it was. But then if that was the case, why didn't my body just stop wanting to cum so much? If that was the case why did my body and my dripping sexuality not agree? It didn't stop wanting. It didn't stop the urges in me to cum. And more than that - the need and the want and the angst just got more and more so. "You see Tara, you have got a lot to learn and I am going to teach you. I'm going to teach you and Rob - well, he will have an input from time to time if that makes sense." Oh I got it alright, her sarcasm didn't escape me even if my mind was melting. I had the feeling that she meant that Rob's input would be to slip his cock into any of my available orifices at any time that she, or he deemed appropriate. I got it because she was speaking with a slight smile on her face. And I got it because I was supposed to get it.

And the thought didn't completely repulse me. In fact, if he put his cock back into me right at this moment it would have been ok. Those infernal beads inside me. I didn't think I could get any more aroused but I was wrong. And Geena was just tracing her finger nail around my sex lips. The thing was that I seemed more sensitive down there now. It seemed like I was hypersensitive down there and the slightest touch, even the slightest touch with one of Geena's nails would send reverberations deep inside my wide-open receptors. I kept having to suck the drool back. I think, as I was feeling then, if I was going to be humiliated or degraded about anything then that was it. That I couldn't control my own saliva and drool. Geena would play her fingers a certain way, say she would trace a nail around the outer edges of my outer lips and she would watch me. She would watch for my reactions and she would 'really' watch. And then she would adjust her touch. Just micro adjustments that I am sure that I wouldn't normally be aware of. But in this hyper state of sensitivity and awareness I was aware of everything.

And I could feel my sexual muscles working - or at least trying to work with her fingers. I knew that it was my body being greedy and if anything, I was aware that that was something else that I should have been humiliated about. Being greedy and being needy like that. That should have made me feel humiliated and ashamed of myself. But I was too young then. Too young to get the humiliation and the degradation as part of a sexual scene. Or part of the cruelty. That was too deep for me. I did feel a bit 'stupid' that I couldn't control my mouth and my drool. There was this constant need for me to suck it back and when I did this my mouth made some obscene noises. I guess this was all stuff that I should have been feeling guilty and humiliated about. But that would come later. That would come once my mind got used to being where it was supposed to be. Once my mind and body accepted this thing that was happening to me then I would have more time to think. Because I wouldn't be so bemused and because my inbuilt defences wouldn't be trying to fight what was happening to me. I didn't know all of this then. All I knew was what was happening to me at this time. All I knew was that I was trying to make sense of it at the same time as trying to deal with my enhanced sexuality.

"Why don't you get down on your hands and knees Tara. Let's get you 'posed' and nice. This is something you will need to get used to. This is something you will need to adjust to - being 'posed' for others to see. And being posed for others to use. Its ok, you will get used to it though. You'll get used to it and you will crave it." What the fuck was she on about? She sounded like a nutcase! And yet at the same time as she was talking in these whisper like ways, she was trailing her finger nail up and down my slit. God, my slit, my sex slit was so wet. In fact, it wasn't that it was wet any more, it was saturated and it was as though my sexuality, my cunt, was in some kind of slow eruption. That eruption being my juices. Bubbling, oily, slippery juices that were just erupting from me slowly. Continuously pouring from me. Pouring down from my sex to the valley between my ass cheeks. And what was helping that flow was the constant movement of my sexual muscles. Making it appear that my sex was alive and breathing. The undulating, the constant peeling apart of my sex lips and the pushing out of those juices as though my cunt was doing that all by itself.

What did she even mean that I would be 'posed'? I was about to find out as I managed, somehow to get down onto my hands and knees. That was no easy feat. I was so weak and wobbly from the arousal. My usual demeanour was confident. I could even do high heels but this night I was a wreck. It was funny really, I was a wreck and I knew I was. But it didn't matter. With every movement I made, even the smallest of movements, I was reminded of my sexual state. And I was reminded of those beads inside me. By this time I was naked. I should have been bothered about being naked with this woman - and even more bothered about what she was doing to me. But the truth was that I wasn't bothered at all.

All I was bothered about was how I would handle the feeling of wanting to cum and needing to cum but not being allowed to cum. Having to move didn't help. I had to manage to get up from the recliner and then get down to my hands and knees. I should have been telling this woman to fuck off and that I wouldn't do it. That would have been it in the ideal world. But the truth was that I was in her world. She had taken me into her world and now she was getting ready for the long haul of taking me deeper and deeper.

I let out some kind of noise. Like a wet, drooling groan as I got to my hands and knees. My pussy was in some kind of spasm. Not a painful spasm but one that sent a series of hyper pleasure pulses through me. Those little bursts of pleasure stopped me in my tracks. I had to take a moment. And I had to take deep, deep breaths. It wasn't fair. I could feel those pleasure pulses, I could experience them but I wasn't allowed to do what would be the most natural thing for me to do and orgasm. I knew that I could have orgasmed. It wouldn't have taken much. I could have just waited for another series of those pleasure pulses and then squeezed the beads that were buried inside my bottom - that would have tipped me over for sure. But at the same time, I knew that I couldn't do that. I daren't do that. Just for a split second the question of what Geena could do if I came and came and came? I was thinking, 'what the fuck could she do to me?' But there was something inside me telling me that I couldn't do that. That I had better not do that. It was like there was something around a blind corner that would be deeply unpleasant for me if I went against her instructions. I didn't even know how this was a humane way of one woman treating a younger woman. I mean, how could I be in the position? I know for one thing, my mum was further from my mind than she had ever been. I had quite enough to contend with.

I cried out again when I was on my hands and knees. The sheer undiluted pleasure had just made me hunch up and hang my head forward. And in doing that the drool had simply spilled from my mouth and to the floor. But at the same time the vagina drizzle was pouring from my sex as well. I was leaking and drizzling and drooling from both ends of me. "Oh no, no that will not do at all. Not at all." That was Geena again. She was over me now and she kept walking past me, past my line of vision. Her in high heels and her legs sheathed in the most expensive nylon. "You need to retain as much dignity as you can, for as long as you can because it will be gone soon enough." And that was the first real time that I had thought about dignity, and humility and the losing of them. She had fed the words to me in such a way that I had had to think about them. I had had to associate them with this predicament that I was in. I can't say anything other than I was being driven mad with what was going on. I knew about being sexy and horny. And I knew about needing to go and 'sort myself out'. As teenagers we joked about it all the time. We often had been in fits and fits of laughter. Especially me and Candice. It was because we didn't really understand. It was because it was all rude and it was all coming to us - that we were growing up and having to deal with grown up things. But this was something different. Something so different that there are no words.

"Hold your head up. Spread your knees wide and dip your back. Let the natural concave curve of your back be seen." What she really meant was dip my back so that my ass was thrusting backwards. And what she really meant was spread my knees so that my slippery, drizzling sex could be seen. And what she really meant was hold my head up high and let your face be seen. Let the state of me be seen. What she really meant was that there was no hiding place for me. That 'posing' like this meant that I was on display. That I was there for her to see. And for Rob to see and for all I knew, anyone else to see. That was what Geena really meant when she was giving me those posing instructions. But I didn't care. I just didn't care about what she wanted me to do. All I cared about was what was going on between my legs and inside my mind. That was all I cared about. And I know now that Geena knew what state my mind was in. And I know that she knew the state of my sexuality and need. I wasn't in this place in this state by accident. She had taken me here.

And then she was running her fingernail down the centre of my spine. Like she was emphasising the dip in my back. Almost like she was 'approving' of that dip in my back. Starting at the nape of my neck and then coming down. Slowly. Just tracing my spine and sometimes going back, retracing then coming down further and further to the bit just above my tail bone. The trouble was that her doing that like that was making me squeeze on those beads inside me. And when I did that I was trembling with the pleasure pulses that I was giving myself. "You sex is moving. Its opening and closing, opening and closing." Geena was speaking as though it was something obscene that I was doing to myself. I know now that the way she was speaking, what she was doing, giving me hard knocks like this was deliberate. What she was saying wouldn't mean much to me when I was in such a heightened state of sexual need, but later, at a time when I was brought down from that, at a time when I was prevented from giving myself those pleasure pulses, and at a time when I had plenty of time to think, her words would come back to me. And that would be when the hard hit wold occur. That would be when I would be made to realise what she wanted me to realise.

I seemed to be posed like that for a long time. On my hands and knees, my head high, knees wide and back dipped. And during that time, I could feel Geena's eyes on me. "You need to get used to feeling eyes on you Tara. There will be a lot of eyes on you." And she was telling me this as drool, as though elasticated drool was stretching down to the floor from the corners of my mouth and from the centre of my bottom lip. Likewise, between my legs except the drool from my cunt was thicker. It still stretched unbroken to the floor, but it was thicker more mucous like. But that was the vision of me that Geena had and enjoyed. All the time my anal muscles were squeezing and then releasing those beads inside me and that provided more visual enhancement for this woman. "Please Geena, please can I cum, please. Please Geena?" I hadn't planned on asking for permission to orgasm. Not at all. And I was surprised to hear to come from between my drooling lips. It was as though it was someone else who was asking on my behalf. It must have been that inner desperation - that

98

inner 'need' for me to cum. And that was it, the 'need' it was a need so pure and so real that only begging, in the tone that I begged would do.

"If you're a good girl Tara. I mean if you are a really good girl then I may, I 'may' let you cum. But not yet." There it was again. The good girl thing again. I heard the words but they were just grating on my nerves. Geena's words were shredding my nerves. I didn't think she understood how desperate I was to cum but then I knew that she did understand at the same time. Fact was that I was on the edge. On the edge of cumming yes but also on the edge of madness. I didn't know how much longer I could go without spilling into orgasm. "Anything Geena, anything. I'll do anything." What I was saying was huge but I meant every single word of it. I would do literally anything just to be allowed to cum. There was this pause and I heard Geena let out a huge sigh. I didn't know what that was all about at the time. But I know now that me saying that would have been a huge gratification for her. Like a sexual kick. Me in this state and promising that I would do 'anything' to be allowed to cum. "I know you will Tara. I know you will. But for now, what I want you to do, is just 'push' push with your ass and eject those beads I put up there one at a time. Take your time. Just do one, then stop then wait for me to tell you to do another. Do that all the way until you don't have any left. But you are NOT allowed to cum. I repeat you are NOT allowed to cum. Think you can do that for me sweetie? If you do it - if you manage to do it exactly as I have just told you - well then I will consider letting you cum."

That was what registered the most - that Geena would consider letting me cum. That if I did as she was telling me then she would consider letting me cum - so there was hope there. What did not register was the task at hand. How hard it would be to push those beads out

99

and not cum. How difficult that would be. How 'impossible' it would be actually. I only got to know how hard it would be when I came to eject the first bead. I had to struggle to stop squeezing and to adjust myself into the 'pushing' out of that first bead. The first bead being the last one that was put inside me. Geena was behind me - she was right down there and she was holding the end of the string that the beads were all connected to. And she was watching. I was pushing but I soon learnt that the pushing action was creating more pleasure, more edge of orgasmic pleasure than the squeezing of my anal muscles created and that was making me whimper. The first one came out pretty easily but I was still panting. But the fact was that each subsequent bead was harder and harder to push out. That was because I had to push each one further down my anal tract to my anus. It took more effort. It took more of a push and therefor it gave me more and more intense pleasure. And that was the thing. It was the more intense pleasure with each bead that I ejected. It made my progress slow. In my mind I wanted and needed to get those beads out of me quickly so that I could follow up on the possibility of being allowed to cum. But my progress was slowed because I had to recover between each bead that I ejected out of me.

And that was the thing, I did have to recover. I was panting, and drooling. The drool was spilling from me at both ends. I doubt that I looked dignified. In fact, I know now that I didn't. But I didn't care. I just didn't care. And I know that I was sobbing by the time the last couple of beads left the confines of my anal tract. That last but one bead nearly saw me spill into a forbidden orgasm. It took me a long time to recover from that one. A long time before I could go through the motions of ejecting the very last bead. But I failed on the last bead. I got so far into the ejecting process, and then I just couldn't stop myself. It was like my body gave up - like my mind gave up and I came and came and came. That orgasm reached new heights in intensity and I almost passed out. I didn't quite pass out, but almost. And when I became compos mentis again, I knew that the orgasm I had had was forbidden. It should not have happened. And as I came down from that orgasm realisation was dawning on me that I would probably have to pay dearly for that unauthorised orgasm.

Chapter 11

Two days later

Tina wouldn't know how long she had been sobbing for. Time didn't mean anything now. It was obvious and clear that Tara was in some kind of trouble, and that she could do nothing about it at all. She could feel her lips all cracked. She must have got lost in her own despair for hours. Yes it was hours. She looked at the clock it was 2pm. She had a bizarre thought that Tara would normally have been home about ten or eleven hours ago and if she had been it would all be ok now. But that just started her crying again. She sniffed - her banging headache hadn't gone away. In fact it was worse. When she had dressed herself up earlier she had begun to feel, not good, but better. She had been convinced that Tara would call or message, or something. But then when that call did come from Tara's phone, it was like she was struck with some kind of dreaded nervous disease or something.

She tried to pull herself together but that was a mission in itself. She felt so helpless. In a way it was like she was suffering from some kind of grief for her missing daughter or something. It was like she had 'lost' her for good. But that wasn't the case at all. But that call had spooked her. It had more than spooked her. It had scared her shitless. And whereas before the call she would have had options - like call the police or not, now she didn't have those options because they had been taken off her. They had been taken away from her. That short phone call had changed everything. It had more or less torn her world apart. Instead of being able to do something, she could do nothing. She had to wait - she had to sit and wait it out and that made her feel more than helpless. And it sure simply helped her along to opening another bottle of wine. And it certainly helped to convince her that starting on that new stash of coke was a good idea. More than good idea. And that was what she did. She got the stash out, got all of her tools and paraphernalia again and she sat by the glass coffee table so that she didn't have to get up again. And she could just sit there and do line after line.

She sat with her phone near her in case that person called again - and she had everything she needed in order to get her through this. All she could do was sit there, and wait. She threw her head back against the sofa seat again and closed her eyes. She wished she could stop her head from overworking but she couldn't do that. She had so many threads that she had on the go at the same time it was like her mind, like her brain was on fast forward or something. She felt like she was a mess so she must have looked a mess. She just wanted out of the way she felt. She wished there was an out but she knew there wasn't one. Then she dared to think of just opening the door and walking out. Not just walking out but walking away. Away from everything. But that would mean leaving Tara and she couldn't do that. In her mind she berated herself for even thinking about it. That made her feel guilty on top of everything else she had to contend with. And then she could feel it coming on again. She could feel herself sinking into those memories of her past days again. Into memories and the nightmares of what she had to do to get by. This time it wasn't the Muslims. This time it was the 'real' perverts. The real sadistic bastards. This time it was all about the ones that did what they did, not because it was their culture but because perversion and deviance was what they lived for. It was what they did. But better this than her think about what this other person, this other woman was doing with her Tara.

There was this man. Oh god this man. Tina's flesh crawled when she thought about him. He was a creep. Just one look at him and anyone would get the same impression. Especially the same first impression. Maybe his mother wouldn't have got that impression but then this man was so old, he was so advanced in years that it was unlikely that his mother was anywhere around. Tina thought about this man only with shudders. Even the sight of this shuffling man would make her shudder. Maybe that was because he was so slow, so cumbersome in everything he did because of his advancing years that what he then went on to do didn't sit right in the mind. He used to snap latex surgical gloves on in a way that would tell anyone that the sound of that 'snapping' latex against his wrists turned him on. But also that he knew that such a sound would put Tina, or any of his latest 'victims' more than on edge. He would slip his rubbered fingers inside Tina. Use her own juices as lubrication and then slip them up inside her. And that was what would creep Tina out. The way he was so close to her as he did that. The way she would have to sit on the edge of a table and spread her stockinged legs wide for him as he snapped on his gloves. And then stay like that as his slipped, one, two then three of his digits inside her. And all of the time his warm, almost rancid breath would be washing over her.

In lot of ways, lots of times she had wished this man would just fuck her and get it over with. But he never did that and that was because he couldn't. Whenever Tina slipped into her memories like this she realised that she never saw this man's cock. It was probably a shrivelled up piece of useless flesh. That was what she got at least a little bit of pleasure thinking about. In a way that thought was the only one that got her through back in the day. This man was a regular - once or twice a month, so she would know when his day or his session was coming. He used to insist that she put on a beauty spot, or a mole with her makeup. It was like he wanted this particular look and Tina got the impression that he wanted her to look like someone from his past. That she was actually this person. That this man wasn't doing these despicable things to her, but that he was doing them to this other female that she was dressed and made up to look like. In more than a lot of ways Tina got the feeling that this man was a former sex offender. That he did things to minors. There was nothing ever said, nothing ever mentioned but it was just the overall feeling that Tina had. That and the way that she had to be for him. She would have to suck her thumb as he slipped his rubbered fingers into her. And there were times when she would have to make herself cry but still sit there with her legs spread open for him.

It was as though she was a hybrid for him. She was in stockings, and heels and makeup. And yet she had to act like this 'girl child'. It was like his mind was so fucked up that it couldn't decide what his kink was. Or more like this man was so sick in the head that he wanted the best of all worlds. And the amount of times that Tina had to see this man over the years told her that he had found everything he wanted in her. That was not good for her. In fact, it never bode well that she had to see him so often. And what he did to her and what he made her do she tried and tried to block out of her mind. There were times when she wished she could check into some place to have her memories erased. She would have the memories of this man and what he did erased that was for sure. But she would have the Muslim memories erased as well. She would have done anything for this to be a possibility. Tina was pulled, and dragged out of her back thoughts by her phone ringing.

At first, she didn't know where she was again. And then she didn't get it that her cell phone was ringing and that Tara's number was flashing up on the touch screen. But then she seemed to pull it all together. She snatched up the phone and pressed answer. "Tara, Tara is that you. Tell me where you are I'll come and get you? Just wait there, I will be there as soon as I can." It was like a forlorn hope that she spoke with into the phone. The hope that it would actually be Tara on the other end of the line. In the event, of course, it wasn't. "Hello Tina. It's me again. I just wanted to have a little chat, let you know that Tara is doing very well. She's doing very well indeed. Let's just say that she is coming up to expectations and in some ways exceeding those expectations." It was that woman's voice again. Of course it was Geena, except that her voice had been fed through some sort of electronic filter device that made it sound different. It was still undeniably a female voice, but it had been altered slightly. Maybe this was a first sign that Geena's security or her I's and t's were not so dotted and crossed after all. Maybe a first sign or not, of a woman obsessed with her own security. Whatever, Tina didn't recognise the voice. Not really. She just had this feeling of familiarity with it. It was a strange thing for her. Listening to this voice and having half a feeling that she knew the person. And yet not at the same time.

"Listen to me you fucking piece of shit bitch. You let my girl go now and I might, I might just not hunt you down and kill you slowly and painfully." Tina heard her own words coming out of her mouth and she was shocked. It was as though it had all come on top of her all at once. And it was as though talking into the phone and hoping that it was going to be Tara and then finding that it wasn't was the tipping point. There was more than anger in her voice. She almost hissed out the words. And there was nothing on the other end of the phone except silence. Instantly she was regretful of what she had done. Then there was a click and the phone was hung up. And

Tina was even more sorry that she had let her emotions get the better of her. She just sat and looked at the phone. It was all she could do. She sat looking at it in her wine and coke filed haze and she was willing it to spring back to life. But it didn't do that, not straight away. It was as though Geena was making her sorry for what she had just said. It was as though she was going to make her more sorry than she had ever been. She didn't call back not in five, or ten, or fifteen minutes. Not even in thirty minutes and Tina thought she had screwed up. Properly screwed up.

After forty-five minutes the call came. This time Geena didn't give Tina an opportunity to say anything at all. "Don't say anything, just listen. Like I said, Tara is doing well. She is different to what you will remember, but she is doing well. But I know that I have to talk to you about her future and so we have to talk." Tina was listening but she was having a real problem processing the words that she was hearing. To her, it felt as though this woman was spelling out that she didn't have any right to Tara anymore. That there was a bigger picture involved that Tina didn't have any ownership of or control over. "I mean, you wouldn't want her to end up like you now would you Tina. You like your wine. You like your coke. And you've, how can I put it, you've been the source of gratification to many men, and women, through the years." It was like to Tina that she had been picked up and put on a different planet in a different solar system. "Just, just a second. Look I'm sorry for that outburst, I really am. But who the fuck do you think you are? I don't know you. You don't know me. And you have my little girl and are talking like that it's all ok. That as long as we do things your way there will be no problems. Are you completely and totally 'mad' or what? You have to be?"

Tina's voice was incredulous. That came through in the tone of her voice. There was this baffled bemusement that she couldn't shake off. She carried on. "Ok ok, you just tell me how we are going to get over this situation. You have kidnapped my daughter and in doing so have broken so many laws that you will spend a long, long time in prison. I on the other hand haven't done anything wrong and now I have you on this phone, on my daughter's phone and you want to talk to me about HER future! Please tell me this is a fucking joke, Please!" Tina had turned down her volume but the incredulity was there. Geena was clever in what she did. She didn't jump straight in to defend herself or what she was doing. She let there be another silence and that silence was telling Tina that what she was doing was perfectly alright. It was a mind fuck. Or at the very least it was a small part of a bigger mind fuck. "I hold all of the cards Tina and I am sure, more than sure, that you will fall into line. I didn't have to call you at all. I didn't have to include you at all. I could have simply vanished Tara and you would never have known. But I didn't do this." And there was Geena making it sound like she was doing Tina a favour. And because of Tina's state of mind, and because of the wine and the coke effect. She was believing it.

"Yes, yes of course. I'm sorry. Of course you didn't have to tell me anything. You don't! Just tell me what we have to do next. I don't care what it is. Just tell me. I want to see Tara. I want to see for myself that she is ok." And there it was, the softening of Tina's voice. She had had it pointed out to her that without these calls from this woman she would have nothing. She would have torn her hair out by now and she would have probably hit the insanity scale long before now. It was slowly dawning on Tina that she should be grateful to this woman on the other end of the phone. Geena would have recognised that and she would have smiled to herself. "Now that is a much, much better tone Tina. Try to remember that you need to stay on good terms with me because the next time I hang up, you will NOT hear from me again. Do I make myself clear?" And this time there was a change in Geena's voice. She was in the process of gaining control of Tina and she knew it. She recognised the submission in there and she knew and timed her reeling in to perfection. "Yes, yes I understand of course I understand. I'm sorry. I'm just worried, that's all. I'm worried about Tara and I need to see her." And there was contriteness in Tina's voice. There was a hint of a break in her voice. One that happens just before someone starts to cry. There was little doubt that Tina was at the end of her tether.

"You have to know that Tars is heading in a different direction Tina. We are taking her away from you but this is your chance to not be out in the cold." And now there was that hint that this woman was not working alone, and that there was this bigger picture. "I'm going to suggest we meet. Somewhere public. We meet and talk. And then I can put your mind at rest more. Not so much at rest, but so that you know more. How does that sound Tina?" To Tina it was like this woman was softening and to an extent that she was giving her what she wanted after all. She took it for granted that Tara would be at this public meeting and she jumped at it straight away. "Just tell me when and where and I will be there." And Geena paused just for maybe a few seconds before she responded to an eager Tina. "Not so fast Tina. Firstly, you don't talk to anyone about this. I mean ANYONE. Is that clear?" Tina was on bubbling point again. "Yes, yes that's clear. I won't talk to anyone, I promise." And Geena smiled to herself again. "Good girl." And that almost stopped Tina's heart on the spot. That 'good girl'. She wasn't a girl and she sure as hell wasn't anyone's good girl. She had had to be a good girl in the past and that didn't conjure up good images from back in the day. That threw her a little bit. More than a little bit.

In fact, hearing this woman say those two words transported Tina back and she wasn't sure what to feel or think about that. She didn't get a chance to respond because Geena was on it. "Come up to the food hall, in the Mall at six this evening. Obviously come alone. But more importantly come and be prepared to listen. Be prepared to listen and learn. Not everything you hear you will like. Not everything you see you will like. But you need to know that Tara is already different. She is already not the girl you know, or knew. Just come with an open mind and I am sure that there can be a thread of peace in your mind." The way Geena spoke, it all encompassed the massive head and mind fuck that was taking place. "Look, look we'll do it your way ok. I just wanna know that Tara is ok, that's all." And Tina didn't say anything else. There was nothing else for her to say. She summed it up in that sentence. She had had difficulty in getting her head round the fact that she wasn't in control. She had been controlled by a pimp in her younger years and she had snatched back that control when she got away from that life and did it her way. But now it was like it was being snatched from her again and she was having difficulty in coping with that. But she was accepting that she couldn't do anything about it. She was accepting that she didn't call the shots. There was a click on the other end. Geena had hung up the call. She hadn't even got Tina's confirmation that she would be there, but then she didn't need it. Of course, Tina would be there.

Chapter 12

Tina was reeling from the call. Completely reeling from it. She put the phone down and looked at it like it had just arrived from another planet. Then she tried to replay what had been said during that call in her mind. She couldn't believe the pure audacity of this woman, whoever she was. How she spoke like it was all normal or something. And how she was expected to simply take it. She couldn't believe how fucked up her world had become in such a short space of time. And that was what had happened. This woman had taken her Tara, and then she had proceeded to fuck up her world. The truth of the matter was that if Tina thought her world was fucked up now, then how she would cope with the reality when that was revealed to her, no-one would know. That reality would be something that would surely tip her over the very edge. For now she just had to get her head round that things were very different now.

She had to come to terms with the fact that Tara had been taken and there was nothing she could do about it except what this woman said. She looked at the glass of wine and then picked it up. She looked at the clock. Three hours or so she would have to leave for the Mall. That kind of sent a bead of 'something' coursing through her central nervous system and it unsettled her. Tina had been through a lot of 'unknowns' in her life, especially back in the day. But this was different. It was so different that she didn't know what to do about it. Or what to think about it. She needed to shower. She needed to change. She needed to get her shit together. The sooner she got to do that the better she would be. The question was, could she get her shit together?

There was one thing from Tina's past that had come back to her. When she used to prostitute herself - both when she was pimped out and when she later struck out on her own, there was this thing that happened to her that she couldn't explain and couldn't get her head round. It was happening now. The extra stiff nipples, and the wetness between the legs. There was nothing wrong with Tina, her sexuality was intact. Maybe there was a thought that at times she was overly sexed, or highly sexed, but the point was that she was alive down there. Alive and kicking. But in times of uncertainty, in times where she was not controlling things - like when she was going into the unknown, she got the stiff nipples. Not just stiff nipples but bullet like nipples. And there was this distant throb in that - like an itch that couldn't be scratched. And there was the wetness between the legs. Not just a slight dampness but a saturated wetness. There had been a time, years ago when she had thought she was properly fucked up because of this.

Oh yes, she had thought there was something wrong with her back then. She had pretty established thoughts that she was some kind of freak back then. And those thoughts were back now. Thoughts that it couldn't be right that her body be aroused like this. And that is what she was, she was aroused. On top of everything else, on top of the sheer worry and anxiety over Tara being held by this person by THESE people, she had this blast from the past to deal with. Now she was sitting at her dressing table looking at herself in the mirror and she was trying to make sense, yet again what was happening. She was failing of course. She would never be able to make sense of all of this. She remembered her pimp once told her how good it was that she was always 'ready' to pleasure the punters. By that he meant, how she was wet down there, and with those huge stiff nipples. And how apparently eager she was to please.

That was different though. She had to go perform sexually then. She was being paid to do what she did and she was good at it. At least that was what people told her constantly. That she was very good at sucking cock - that she was very good at swallowing cum. That she was very good at taking cock up inside her ass and up inside her vagina. Even big cocks she was good at servicing. But what could she tell herself now that she was sitting in front of this mirror? The fact was that she couldn't tell herself anything. She simply had to go with the flow. She had to do what she had to do. In a way, in every way actually, she had had the ability to control things, to have things go her way, taken away from her and now she had to simply go with the flow. She had to go with what she knew best. She had to revert back to the old days. And that was what she did. It was all she could - revert to the days when she felt like this before. When she was aroused like this before. She had to create that vision all over again.

The trouble with all of that was that it added another level of despair to her. It added another level of treble anxiety to her. She would dress and she would make up like she was the hooker of back in the day. It was the only way she could deal with what was going on inside her head. And yet at the same time she was worried beyond belief about Tara. For just a few minutes Tina sat bemused and confused at that dressing table. She didn't know where it had all gone wrong. She didn't know how her world could have been turned upside down like this. But she was then thinking the same as she was layering on the makeup. A pale foundation, dark eyes made to look even bigger than they actually were. Lips lined and coloured deep blood red. Those lips made to look even fuller and thicker than they were in reality. Cocksucker lips.

She used to do something back in the day. She used to rouge her nipples and she used to coat them with a nail hardener. It was just her little spin on things. It was like she used to recognise what caught the eye, and what

113

flicked the switched in men's minds. And she was more than sure even back then that if a man had seen that she had spent time preparing her extremities like this, then she had to be very hot indeed. It was as though the simple act of coating her nipples like this was a very hot thing. And so she had to be a very hot thing. It wouldn't be wrong to say that Tina had been a girl, and a woman who had fulfilled many men's fantasies in many ways. And this is what she did now. She teased her nipples to make sure that they were the hardest they possibly could be and then she rouged them. She rouged them the same colour that she used on her lips. And then she got her nail polish out - a clear lacquer and she carefully, almost sensuously coated each nipple so that the hardness, the stiffness was caught in like a frozen moment in time. Frozen stiff and extra hyper sensitive.

Those nipples were more than visible through the thinness of the silk top that she wore. A silk top that attracted the eyes to the poke through and the sheer size of those nipples. There were occasions, like split seconds that Tina couldn't explain to herself what the fuck she was doing. Or what the fuck she was thinking about doing this. She did another line of coke. At times like this, she knew from the past, the coke helped her through things. Funnily this time though it didn't help the guilt. But then it didn't explain why she didn't dress down. It didn't explain why she didn't put a stop to this dress up session. Maybe that was it. Maybe she was trying to relive the past. Maybe she was so distraught over Tara that she was living as though she were in a dress and makeup session with her one and only. Whatever it showed that Tina was on very thin ice in terms of being rational and in being sane.

She looked at herself in the full length mirror the way she always did when she went out. She did that as much in the days since she had escaped her sleazy life as she had when she was in it up to her neck. She was still a fan of herself. She still knew how good she looked. But looking at herself it was indeed like a blast from the past. She turned on her red soled stilettos and she tried to look at herself from different angles eventually coming back to facing herself straight on. She was all legs, and bust. And of course nipples. Thank god the dampness between her legs was concealed. At least it was concealed for now. But then it hit her. It hit her about Tara.

That this was all about Tara and what the fuck was she thinking, dressing up like this? It was like it had hit her in a moment of clarity. But that was it, a moment of clarity. And then she was back in her role, back in that mode that she had been through back in the day. She considered changing, toning it down but there was this thing inside her that was telling her no. She had got through those sleazy, dirty days by living on her wits, by living by wire, by going with her gut instinct and that was what she had to do now. She looked at the clock. She needed to leave for the Mall.

She drove there. She didn't need to, she could have got a cab. But there was something in the back of her mind was telling her that when she got Tara back, she would want to drive her home. That was the thing that had formulated in her mind. That she would meet this person, this woman, or these people who had taken Tara, that they would then spend some time talking as though civilly because it was in a public place after all. And then her and Tara would leave in one direction and that woman, or those people if she wasn't alone would go the other way. In Tina's mind it was all as simple as that. It was like there was part of her mind that wasn't getting it. Like she wasn't getting the enormity of the situation. In a way it was a shame that she wasn't getting it. It would have been useful if she could have at least had a tiny grasp of the reality that was about to hit her because that

115

was the thing, when the reality did hit her there would be very little defence from it, or for it. Once Tina went in at the deep end, that would be the end of it.

"Ah Tina, pleased you could make it, and on time. I'm impressed." The voice had startled Tina. She had made her way to the top floor of the Mall from the underground car park and she had been in a bit of a world of her own. Still thinking it would all be over in a little while and her and Tara could go home. She stopped in her tracks and looked. For some reason she had expected to know the woman or recognise her from the past or something. But there was no recognition, nothing. She just looked blankly at the woman. "Where's Tara, I want to take her home. I want to take her home now." There had been all sorts of eyes, from all sorts of directions on Tina and what she looked like as she had come through the Mall and then the food court. It was a case of hearing her stilettos before the eyes saw her. But people were turning away now - they had come to their own conclusions about Tina and what she must surely have done for a living and now they were turning away and getting on with their lives. Meanwhile Tina was trying to get on with hers.

"Ah, I'm afraid it isn't as simple as that Tina. Please take a seat, we need to talk." Geena was looking right at Tina but she was indicating to the seat opposite her. To her left the part time mute Rob sat. He was all eyes. His eyes poured all over Tina and one would be sure to see this happening that Rob was imagining what he could do with a woman like Tina. For him, she was a woman who knew what it was all about. She was a woman who knew how it had worked. She had been there done that and got the t-shirt. It was fact that to sexually use and abuse a woman who knew what was happening to them at any given time was more gratifying than doing it to the innocent. The innocents had their place - the bemusement, the crying the sobbing. But to have a mature woman under complete control and abuse was something else. It was like the nectar of domination. And for some reason these thoughts were clearly written all over Rob's face.

Tina sat down and she crossed her legs. There was that sound of nylon on nylon rasping together. Her eyes were flicking round. She was expecting Tara to come join them. She was reasoning that she would sit and she would talk for as long as she needed to, and then her and her girl were getting the fuck out of there. Except it wasn't going to be like that. It wasn't going to be like that at all. "Who are you, what do you want? Where is Tara. I want to take her home now. Enough is enough." It was like her mouth was on some sort of autopilot. "Just relax Tina. Take a deep breath and relax. I'm going to explain things to you. I will take you to see Tara a little later, but there are things you need to understand first and I need to make sure that you understand them BEFORE you see Tara. You have to be prepared to see Tara. You will be shocked so you need to be prepared beforehand. Are you understanding what I am saying to you Tina?"

That was the thing. Geena was talking to Tina as though she was some kind of retard. Tina must have felt like she was in some kind of twilight zone. Like how could this woman be talking like this in this day and age? How could a person encroach on another's life and it all be as though it's the most natural normal thing in the world to do? Tina took a deep breath and she exhaled. "Ok, you asked me to come here, I'm here. I'll listen to what you've got to say, but then I want to go home, with Tara. That is going to happen. I won't speak about this to anyone. I won't tell the authorities about this, but this does end today. I promise you, one way or the other this ends today." Tina sounded plausible. Given her state of mind. Given how much coke she had done,

117

given how much wine she had drunk, given the fact that the woman sitting opposite her was holding her little girl somewhere. And given what this woman was inferring, what she was hinting at.

When she felt Rob's hand on her leg, at first she thought she must have been mistaken. It was only when the hand crept up to her crotch that she knew for sure what she was feeling. If she had been a woman from the normal world, if she hadn't been a woman who had been on the path that she had been on, she would have recoiled from that hand. She might have slapped it away. She might had screamed out in horror. But this was Tina. And it was like in that split second, in that moment in time she was transported to those days when she gratified the most perverse in society. She had been used to having hands all over her body, and fingers inside her. She had been used to all sorts of attention in all sorts of ways that wouldn't be acceptable to someone from the normal world. And for that reason she simply sat. She simply let that hand be on her crossed over leg. And she simply let then hand creep up and down her nylon sheathed thigh. Geena didn't say anything. She knew what was happening. There would have been some kind of signal to Rob for him to do that, so she knew it was happening. But she was watching. And she was making mental notes.

"It isn't going to end today Tina. I have to tell you that. If I didn't tell you that then it would be irresponsible of me." This was a woman going on about irresponsibility! "You need to accept your place in the food chain Tina. Just like Tara has accepted it. And YES, she has accepted her place, trust me. You will see this for yourself. But YOU need to accept yours. Once you accept your place then we can all move on. Tara is different now. In the short amount of time she has been with us, she has come to know, come to learn that she

118

has to live in a certain way. That she has to have constant 'help' to live the way she needs and has to live." Geena was talking and Tina was listening. But once again Tina was confounded by what she was hearing. It was like she had been transported to that other planet and she had so much to learn. What she couldn't get to grips with was the terms in which this woman was talking about Tara. It was just too much for her. She took another deep breath and exhaled. But she didn't say anything.

Geena didn't say anything either for a while. She was just watching Tina. Rob was rubbing the leg now higher and he had found the pale flesh above the stocking top, and he had found the dampness that was affecting the thigh. More to the point Tina knew he had found the dampness. She squirmed a little bit and it was as though this man finding her dampness the way he had kind of qualified what Geena was trying to get through to her. "Am I making myself clear Tina?" She wasn't really making herself clear. But what was happening was that Tina's past was coming back to haunt her. It shouldn't have been and it shouldn't have had any bearing on what was happening right now and what was happening with Tara. But now she was putting it all together as one. And she was kind of accepting this as all being her fault. It was like her mind was scrabbling to re-adjust but in that re-adjustment was the acceptance. She didn't say anything, she just nodded and when she did that Geena was watching.

"I think you're getting the picture now Tina. I don't need to spell anything out to you. You 'know'. We'll talk about 'your' future in due course, but for now - for now we need to talk about Tara. Tara is central in all of this and before I take you to her, before you see her there are things you need to know." And Geena sat back and crossed her own legs. Tina had uncrossed hers and she had parted her knees a little bit. She hadn't been told to, and she hadn't been coerced into doing so - she just did it so that Rob had easier and better access. She was being the good girl that she used to be in the past.

Chapter 13

Two hours later

Even with the heavy makeup Tina looked pale and withdrawn. There was a 'slump' in her demeanour as she sat on that chair in the food court of the Mall. Rob's fingers had been inside her and were still inside her and he was swirling his fingers around inside her - helping himself to her femininity. And she had expelled her juices all over his fingers and hand. The fact that she had been penetrated like that wasn't the reason that she was pale and slumped in demeanour. Rather it was what she had heard from Geena over the two hours that had taken it out of her. What she had heard had got into her head and fucked with her psyche. She was in shock and that much was plain to see.

If there was a possibility that she could have had her view of her own daughter changed by this woman and what she said then it had happened. It was like she wasn't believing what she had been told, but at the same time not being able to help but to believe it. Or not being able to deny it. What she had been told over two hours had shocked her and rocked her to the core. And yet there was still mother love there. There was still that unconditional love that existed between a mother and daughter that couldn't be broken. Could it? She just had to deal with all that Geena had said to her. All that she had told her. She had to deal with it, take it into her psyche and deal with it. That was what was made her look pale and withdrawn. That was what had made her look like a beaten defeated woman. She was shocked to the core and she had to deal with it. If she could!

There was just too much for her to take in and she was trying to fight it but with no success. "I'm going to take you to see Tara now Tina. I think you need to see

121

her for yourself. Just so that you can put all of what I have told you into context. I think it will be easier once you've seen her for yourself." And there was that spark of hope left in Tina. She was going to see Tara. It might be alright after all. Maybe it wasn't as black a picture as she was painting herself. Maybe it wasn't as black as this woman was making it sound either.

She was making it sound like Tara was a no-hope case. As though she was beyond the point of any return or beyond the point of any help. If this woman was to be believed Tara was like some sort of freak who would need help and assistance to manage her 'condition' for the rest of her life. But she would not be the one to give her that help because she too was beyond the point at which she could give help. She just had to ride this through - that was what she had to do. It would all be ok after that. She would get this day over and it would all be ok. Except it wouldn't be.

"What's that noise?" Geena looked troubled. She actually looked beyond troubled. "That's Tara. She's in distress and that's the only way that she can let it out, to make that noise." The car ride to the house had been more or less in silence. Silence that is except for Rob's hand up and down Tina's leg, and then the squelching sound as he dipped his fingers into her time after time after time. He shouldn't have been allowed to do that but Tina didn't feel she had enough of a reason to stop him. With what she had been told, and what she felt herself she had thought that being a good girl like that was the right thing to do. So, she had sat between the two in the back of that car and she had been given just enough room to part her knees to assist Rob in his assault of her sexuality. "You see Tina, there are certain people in this world that shouldn't be allowed to live in freedom and without restriction. Tara is one of these, and possibly you as well. And that's where people like me come in.

We are here to 'help' these people through life as best as is possible." It had been pretty much all that Geena had said to Tina for the whole trip. She had come out with that line as the man that was sitting the other side of Gina was knuckle deep inside her sex. What was happening was that Tina was having her defences taken away. She was having her psyche worked on.

"But that can't be Tara. It sounds like... it sounds like some kind of animal for gods sakes." Tina's voice was incredulous and she tilted her head trying to get some kind of recognition in the distant noise that she was hearing. She had been taken in to the house from the side entrance. The grander part of the house had been missed. All the way through the back and down into the cellars via the side, or via the tradesmen's entrance. "I know, I know Tina, it's hard to comprehend I know that. But you have to try to prepare you mind for what you're going to see. You have to prepare yourself. I'm not telling you it will be easy. Just be a good girl, and wait here, until I call you in." They were in a dark, low ceilinged hallway in the basement part of the house. Just a single light bulb lit the way. Geena used the 'good girl' as some kind of trigger that Tina would respond to. And it did have that effect. Tina's tongue touched the corner of her glossed mouth and she stood.

Geena disappeared through a door. As she had opened the door there had been an escape of that noise that Tara made. It made her mother visibly shudder. The noise which largely was indescribable had been filtered by that door, but when it opened there was the full brunt of that noise. And Tina had been right, it did sound animalistic. It sounded like an animal in distress. One caught in a trap perhaps. Or one so distressed that this noise was the only way it could let its distress be known. To Tina that wasn't her girl that she could hear. It was as though she was in denial that that noise could possibly

123

be coming from Tara. Tara was a happy go lucky, beautiful young woman about to burst into full womanhood. And that noise did not represent her at all. There had been another noise as the door slammed closed on a strong spring. Tina shuddered again. It was like her mind was torn between letting her believe that it was Tara and letting her be in complete denial. Like she was caught in some kind of fucked up no man's land.

It seemed like Geena was gone for a long time. During that time the noises coming from beyond the door died down. There were noises but not such distressed noises. Rob had been pressed into Tina and he had been feeling her tits. Tina was being a good girl because it was what she knew. She was standing so that he could help himself - she was assisting him in a way. Her psyche was wired up that way, and Geena had taken advantage of her weakness to enhance the way she felt about herself. Rob played with her breasts and with her coated nipples because he could. He did it in a way that would tell anyone that he had every right to do that - and that was what Tina felt. Then the door opened again. There was a noise that came out. Like a rustling noise. But there was also a heady wave of hot air. And within this hot air there was this smell - this aroma that simply hit one in the face and then clung to the face. It was a smell, and aroma that Tina was familiar with but she couldn't place it. It was as though she recognised it from the past but she couldn't quite remember.

"Come in Tina. Come see your little girl." Geena used words that were emotive deliberately. Come see your little girl! Like words that would pluck the heartstrings of any mother. And just for a moment like a split second there was this hesitance in Tina. This was the point that she would see her girl again but there was that uncertainty about what she would see the other side of that door. She took a step but then stopped. It seemed

124

that Geena had done as good a number on Tina as she had on Tara. "It's ok I'm with you the whole way. Take your time, there's no rush. You know you won't be able to 'unsee' what you are going to see now so it's important that you are prepared." And it was like Geena was using every trick in the book, taking every opportunity to fuck with Tina's head. There was the click click click of Tina's high heels. Oddly the clicks stopped the moment that Tina stepped into the room. And when she did step in the door slammed shut but there was this other noise that leaked out. There had been a moment's silence, just pure silence and then there had been this other noise. That wasn't Tara, that was her mother trying to absorb deep shock that she had just been inflicted with.

It had taken a little while, a few seconds for Tina's eyes to get used to the red tinged light that existed in that room. Her hand had gone to immediately cover her mouth and nose to protect herself from the stench. She knew what the stench was. It was rubber. Latex rubber. Her high heels hadn't clicked because the floor was coated in rubber. The walls were also covered in rubber and the ceiling were covered in rubber. There was no immediate source of the red light viewable. This lighting was concealed and provided a 'glow'. It had taken just that little while for Tina to become accustom to this environment. Then her eyes were drawn to a noise from the centre of the room. Geena watched the mother as realisation dawned on her. She watched her eyes open wide, and then her mouth. And it was as though this woman, this ex prostitute, this 'good girl' was in a silent scream.

Tara takes the story up again

The only way mum would recognise me is from the high tight pony tail that erupted from the crown of the rubber hood. That rubber hood was also a mask that covered and clung to my face. It was so tight, so 'fitted' that it was like a second skin. I know that if the light was different mum would recognise my rubbered features. But it was that dull red glow. Geena had been good enough to turn down the internal vibration for mum's entrance into my cell. Geena called this room a cell, my cell because she said that it would be home for me from now on. I wanted Geena to turn down that vibration but I didn't at the same time. I needed the orgasm. I needed the never-ending orgasm that had all but fucked up my mind. But Geena was giving me some dignity back. Not a lot of it, just a little bit for when mum came in and saw me. I'm not sure if this was Geena being kind or whether in her own twisted way she was being even more sadistic. She could have left the vibration to my clitoris and to the inner walls of my vagina, and my nipples, and she could have let mum see me all in one hit.

I guess that way it would be all over too soon. If she let her see the state of me and hear the state of me all in one go, then the shock would be lessened. But if she turned it all down, which she did, and let me be at least partially stable, then she could get used to seeing me like this before the main event. I kind of knew by now how Geena's mind worked. She had taught me and she had brought me to where I am now. I tried to get my breath. I'd didn't know how long that permanent orgasm had gone on for. It was impossible for me to think of anything when that was happening to me. Nothing else had any bearing on what my mind and body was feeling. But I had needed to get my breath. To get my poise back again because there was no poise or dignity when that beautiful sensation took over my whole rubbered body.

126

I couldn't know what mum saw. Or how her mind processed what she was seeing when she stepped into my cell. I was aware she was there. My senses since Geena had been helping me, were super aware. Hyper aware in fact. The shiny black rubber cat suit that I had been fitted with had this occlusive effect. It kind of isolated me from reality. She would see the shine of this skin-tight rubber suit. She would see this figure, me, with her feet and legs slightly deformed from standing on ballet heeled boots that were tight fitting and knee length. Those boots forcing me onto my very tip toes. The resulting arch in my spine forcing a stance that was far from natural. I was used to those heels but not used to them at the same time. Geena told me that I had to be enhanced like this. That it would be good for me in the long run. She said that girls like me needed to be enhanced and emphasised to the maximum. I had seen what I looked like because Geena had wheeled a huge mirror so that I could see myself on the raised platform in the centre of my cell. I was shocked by what I looked like. I knew that mum would be as well. The rubber, the heels, the stance I was forced to adopt in those boots. I knew it would shock her. It had shocked me so god only knows what it would do to mum.

I don't know what I thought when she made that noise. When she realised it was me. I knew she would recognise the hair. It was the only bit of 'me' Tara that was viewable. There were my stretched sex lips, and my throbbing, rock hard nipples that were like torments to me. My sex lips had been stretched but so too had my clitoris. That bundle of eight thousand nerve endings pulled and stretched through slits in the otherwise sealed rubber. She wouldn't recognise me from those pieces of flesh. But when she put it all together in her mind, when she added it all up she was getting her worse fears her worse nightmares coming true. I can't describe the noise that mum made any more than she would be able to describe the din that I would make in front of her when the vibrations inside me were turned back on.

I only had a little bit of space in which to move on those boots. That was because I was chained to the platform. Geena had told me that girl like me had to be chained up and that eventually it would all make sense to me. So, my steps were hobbled and that didn't help my stance. It was a constant effort. Every time I did move there was the creak of latex. And the silent 'clicks' of metal tipped high heels on the rubber floored platform. I'm not sure what it is about latex and rubber. The whole rubber thing. Geena tells me that rubber is good for me because it keeps all the bad in and the good out and that it's what I need right now. It is weird - this rubber. It has a weird effect. It helps my arousal levels - helps to keep them up and I don't know how or why. Even now with the vibrations turned off, I am dripping with arousal. I am always dripping. Mum won't have seen the dripping straight away, but when she made that soul-searching noise she would have seen it. Or just before.

"Why... why have you done this to her? Why?" Mum's voice was disbelieving. I knew it would be. "It's for her own good Tina. She needs to be controlled and she needs to be in a certain state, all the time. It's for her own good." I was starting to believe that. What Geena said to mum and what she said to me made sense. It all made sense. No normal girl would be like me and Geena was helping me. She was good like that. To be honest I don't know what I would do without her. And I knew that mum would have to get her head around it as well. I knew she would be shocked and upset. And I'm sorry about that but she needs to know how I have to live from now on. I don't know how she will cope with that. From that forlorn noise that she made I don't think it will be easy for her. But then it wasn't easy for me either. I had

128

tried to rebel when Geena first came on the scene. But I don't do that anymore because she has taught me the error of my ways. And she has taught me that she is helping me and that I should be grateful for that. And I am!

Just when the noise from mum was dying down, just when she was getting her head round what she was seeing and how she was seeing me, her little girl, Geena turned the vibrations back on and the effect in me was instant. There was no build up, there was no preparation of the body or the mind - all that occurred was undiluted, pure orgasm as I stood, or tottered on those ballet heels. There was a gush of air from me. My deep red lips were outside the rubber, just like my nipples were and just like the lips of my sex and the centre of my sex, my clitoris was. I can't explain or describe even being in permanent orgasm. It's like there are no words. Everything else just pales into insignificance and all that matters is that pleasure. That pure pleasure. The drip from between my rubbered legs becomes like a gush. And that gush like the orgasm is constant. Nothing else matters, not even my mum who has seen the change in me and is making another level of noise. I am making the noises I am making because of the pleasure that my body and mind is having to contend with. That's why mum would have thought before she saw me that I was some kind of animal in distress.

I do take steps on those heels. I have to. Keeping still and standing on one spot during the orgasm is not an option. It's not an option because I don't have enough control to keep still. As that hyper pleasure rushes through every fibre of my body my movements are involuntary. I sob out loud but only because the pleasure is so beautiful. It really is so beautiful but at the same time it is tortuous as well. I'm aware of mum just looking on with her jaws agape as I ride the orgasm and keep riding it. I keep riding it because it is constant. It is a constant orgasm. Geena says I need this. I need to learn and know what is important to me now and that is 'orgasm'. I believe her. I already know it. Now mum has to learn it and know it.

Chapter 14

Through it all I could see my mum. She was just standing there looking at me through the red glow. There was this look on her face that I had never seen before. I thought I had seen every facial expression my mother could make but I was wrong. It was like she was seeing a ghost. She was looking right at me. She was looking right at all of me and that was strange. It was like she was trying to process what she was seeing but at the same time was not having much luck with that. Her eyes were all over my rubbered form and she was trying to 'get it'. She was trying to get what she was seeing. Her hand was up to her mouth. That could have been because of the stench of the rubber - I know it was strong in that room. That was another constant that was in that room. It was almost like a 'rubber atmosphere' in there. I know that. It had taken me a long time to get used to that. But now, it was like I wouldn't be able to do without it any more than I could do without Geena. But mum was holding her hand up there like that, to her mouth to hold in the cries of despair and anxiety. I knew that as well. But I knew also that she would get used to seeing me like this. She had to, she didn't have a choice in that. She had to get used to seeing me like this.

But I knew as well that mum would be distraught and destroyed by what she was seeing. She might accept it, eventually, but it was what damage the process of that acceptance would leave behind. Mum was seeing me, her one and only secured to that raised platform, standing on tippy toes and yet with my steps severely hobbled. Simple bondage but effective bondage. Each of my ankles secured to little eyes in the raised platform. And another length of chain between my ankles. The chains to the platform eyes restricted how far I could move on the spike heeled ballet boots and the chain between my ankles restricted the size step, or strides that I could take. In either case the restriction was severe and it affected all of me constantly.

Mum wouldn't have liked that for a start. She wouldn't have liked the way my long legs couldn't do what they were supposed to do. She wouldn't have liked that I was debilitated in any way. I was her little girl after all. I should have been allowed to move and grow and blossom unhindered and without despair. She didn't get it yet. She would eventually get it that I didn't deserve to live like normal girls. She would eventually get it that I had to live this way. That it was the only way that someone like me could be allowed to live. I kind of hoped that it wouldn't be too long before mum got it. I kind of hoped that the penny would drop sooner rather than later.

But that was the thing. There was just so much that she had to take in. "What is happening to her, why is she making that sound again." I heard her asking Geena the question. I wished I could answer it myself. If I had been able to answer it then I could have put it into words that mum would have understood. We spent, or we had spent a long time talking and we kind of understood each other like only a mother and daughter could. But that was the thing, I wasn't allowed to answer, or talk to her. I had been taught that I could only speak when spoken to and even then, only with permission. It was one of the life changing things that I had to live and abide by. "She's orgasming. Multiple orgasms one after the other. One blending into the next and the next and the next. It's something that she needs to do. She needs to do it all the time. It's what she lives for now."

Geena spoke as though this situation was all normal. I know it's not normal. I know it can never be normal but I have accepted it. In my hobbled stumbles, and between those noises that I had to make as a release

132

I was watching mum as Geena spoke to her. Mum had been pale before but she just got more pale. It was like she was in this dream, this very bad dream that she was waiting to be woken up from. And it was as she'd realised what she had just been told that mum changed. I don't know what it was. I cannot put it into words. There was just like this shadow that crossed her face and her expression changed. There was still the horror, there was still the mother love and the inability for her to do anything to help me, but there was also something else. She was looking at me different. It might have been my imagination, it might have been the dull red glowing light playing tricks on my mind, but I thought I could see disgust on her face as she looked at me. Like a pure disgust and that said a lot given mum's background and how she had lived her life. Or the early part of it any way before she had got back on the right track.

Mum seemed to be focussed on the stretched and weighted sex flesh that had been pulled through tight rubber slits between my legs. And she was just looking. She was just looking at my flesh trying to work out what she was seeing. She could see the dripping. I knew she could see the slippery wet stuff just dripping from me. I knew what she could see and I felt ashamed because of that. There was this shame and this guilt that was flowing through me. It was ok though because Geena told me that I would feel that. What she had said about this day was exactly how it was happening. Geena is good like that. She knows things and she helps me through things. "Your mother will be disgusted with you Tara. She will be visibly disgusted with you." That is what she had said and that is what had happened. She had been right so right!

Maybe if mum could feel the sensations that I was feeling right at this time then she might understand. Not that she would definitely understand, but she might. If she could just understand what Geena had told her. If she could just process those words that she had been told maybe she wouldn't have that disgust on her face. But then she was looking at my nipples and I kind of understood the look then. It was because my nipples had changed. They were bigger and fatter. And they were longer. And they were hard as a natural state. My nipples didn't become erect, they were just erect as a normal state. And they had been pulled through the little rubber holes. And those holes had squeezed around the nipple bases. What that had done is simply amplified the throbbing that I felt in each nipple. Like a throbbing that started somewhere deep inside each nipple and was then fed up to the nipple tips. I cannot explain or describe it. All I can say is that if felt as though my nipples needed attention. As though they needed a rub, or a little squeeze. I had got used to feeling like that. I had got used to needing to feel attention given to my nipples. It was all part of the need in me - and the greed in me.

But Geena had put me right there as well. "Your teats are part of what makes you needy Tara. That's why they have to be included in this little programme of ours. That's why they have to be treated like this." And I understood that. She had been right all the way through, why wouldn't she be right about this? But I could feel mum's eyes on me. And that look of disgust again. I could kind of sense the kind of things that were going through her head as she stood there with her hand to her mouth just looking at me, just watching what was happening to me. 'How could she let this woman do this to her? What is the matter with her why doesn't she stop her from doing this?' All sorts of questions that she didn't have the answers to. Maybe she would never get the answers but I did know that she would 'get it' in the end. I did know that sooner or later that penny would drop and she would be on the same page as us all. I sort of knew that she didn't have a choice in that. I knew that she would have to get it in order to survive herself.

Rob the mute had come behind mum and he had draped his arms over her shoulders. He was playing with her breasts and with her nipples. I wondered if mum had done that thing with her nipples, the coating them and hardening them the way she used to. She told me she used to do that all the time. I'm sure she did. She looked like she had put in a lot of effort in the way she dressed for meeting Geena. And now Rob the mute was at her. Well, she had to learn and she might as well learn now. It was what I thought. But I only thought that in broken sections because I was trying to deal with this orgasm. This state of orgasm that I was in. And it was a state that I was in. Each time I was put into this state I was grateful to Geena. Grateful and anxious at the same time. Each time I was put into that state it was like I thought I could not possibly experience another high in intense pleasure. But each time I was wrong. Each time I was taken to another higher plane.

It was pure pleasure but it was torture at this same time. If it had been an orgasm which built up then passed as in the normal world then I would have been able to take a breath and recover, but this wasn't like that. This was an orgasm that just happened and was there, inside me. It was inside my sex, it was inside my body, it was possessing my femininity. It was inside my head. And it was infesting every fibre of my being. I don't know how my rubbered legs didn't just give way and collapse under me but they didn't. I could stumble and totter in those severely restricted steps and I could just absorb that orgasm the best way I knew how. I couldn't spend too much time thinking or worrying about how mum was taking it all. She was way down the list of my priorities. Even in front of me with her looking at me the way she was, it didn't matter. I knew at this point that things with

135

my mother had changed. And that they had changed in a way that wouldn't ever see things back the way they were between us. That was even apparent to me but I didn't care. It was the orgasm that mattered. That beautiful thing that was inside me and around me. The thing that was melting my mind.

I had that feeling. That the orgasmic state that Geena had kindly given me, was melting my mind. But I didn't care about that. Whilst mum was being a good girl for Rob the mute, yet more of my brain was being melted by the orgasm. I let out another of those noises. I didn't do that voluntarily. I wished I could have just absorbed that pleasure and share it with no-one. But it seemed that every time my heavily glossed lips parted, that this noise came out and I shared it with everyone in that red tinged room. I know what that noise sounded like. I sounded like a trapped animal. And in a way, I was trapped. Looking back now I know I was trapped. But it was the orgasm that trapped me. Without that I would have wanted to get away. Maybe I would have tried to get away I don't know. But it was the orgasm that trapped me. That addictive tortuous orgasm that made me drip like a tap between the legs. And that made my nipples throb in a way that made them feel like they would explode. Shuffling round that raised platform like a brainless sex addict. That was what my mum was seeing. That was what she was having to process and absorb. That was what she was so disgusted about.

I wouldn't have wanted to be my mum. I don't think I could have processed it. I could only do it because of the orgasm. The state of orgasm. I did feel for mum, having to see what she was seeing but at the same time I had my priorities. And my priorities were to absorb and enjoy that beautiful orgasm. Nothing else mattered not even mum. I guess our perfect life together had to end. And this was how it ended. Me being taken away from

136

her and shown another way in life. Me being shown how I 'should' live my life because of what I was. That was a strange thing, trying to work out 'what I was'. I didn't know. I knew I was different to other girls because Geena had told me. She had instilled that in me. That fact was firmly entrenched inside my melting mind. But 'what I was'. I didn't have an answer, or even a notion of that. I made that noise again only louder and more drool drenched. The orgasmic state I was in had been taken to yet another higher level and my knees almost buckled under me. Not quite but almost. And I could feel mum's eyes on me. I didn't care.

I was in a position of wanting the orgasm to end but not wanting it to end at the same time. There was just too much to absorb. Who would ever think that someone could be given too much pleasure? But that was what was happening to me. I was on an overload of pleasure and that was overloading every single one of my senses. "Why would you do that to a young girl?" I could hear the conversation but I wasn't interested in it. I could hear it word for word like it was in crystal clear clarity - hi definition hi fi. But it didn't matter to me. In a way mum was contradicting her disgust in me. She was showing through her mother love and yet at the same time there was still that look of pure disgust on her face. I was over that. I had much more important things to think about. Or a much more important thing to think about. The orgasm. My state of orgasm. "I'm just helping her realise her true self Tina. I haven't done anything to her. She is just being herself. She is just being what she is. And you have to get used to it. You have to get used to seeing her like this. And what's more you have to fall into line yourself Tina. I mean, Tara got her genes from you. She is from your gene pool and look what has happened to her. Look at her. Just spend a few seconds and look at her Tina. You have to bare some of the responsibility for this. You have to take your bit of the blame for the way she has turned out."

And it was as though those words from Geena had made mum stop in her tracks and look at me more intensely. I could feel her eyes on me. I was hypersensitive to everything in this state. In my dripping orgasmic state I was extra sensitive to everything, even mum's eyes. She was looking me up and down and it was as though Geena's words were hitting home. "How could you say that to me, in front of her. She will hate me?" Mum sounded genuinely hurt but what Geena had said. It was as though her words had really cut into her psyche. It was as though she was being made to realise that she was at the very least, partly to blame for the way I was. She was wrong though to suggest that I would be hurt and shocked to hear all of that. As far as I was concerned Geena was just telling it as it was. She was just telling the truth and to be frank, because of my state of mind and my state of sexuality, I didn't give a flying fuck. I felt detached from mum. Actually, more than detached from her.

"I'm just tell you the truth Tina. Some people don't like the truth. But you know, you have my sympathy in one respect." And Geena stopped talking - as though she were trying to formulate the right words. As though she was being careful to find the right words before she continued. "Why, why would I have your sympathy for anything after what you have done here?" I could hear the anger in mum's voice. Mum didn't get angry at all, very rarely actually and yet she was angry. I could sense that. I didn't care. All I cared about is how I tippy toed in those boots to heighten the next series of mega orgasmic sensations. "I haven't done anything to her. Have you not been listening Tina? You have my sympathy because you have to leave here. You have to leave here later and get on with your life. And that life will never be the same again. And whereas neither will Tara's she will have me to look after her and see her through to the end of her natural life. But you will have to cope all on your own. You will have to live with what you've seen here. You will have to live what you know about Tara's existence now. And you will have to just carry on in the normal world. That might not mean much to you at the moment. But when you're home, later tonight - all alone and you get to thinking. Thinking how your life was and how it will be in the future, then it will hit you."

I had to give it to Geena, she knew how to lay on the despair and the shock when she put her mind to it. She was just telling mum how it was going to be. And I could tell even through my mega orgasm that her words were getting through to mum and that finally she was realising. It was almost as though as mum was trying to imagine herself at home all alone right now. "I know Tina. It's like a punishment in itself, isn't it? I'm guessing you might have thought that I would take you in as well as your little girl. But that won't happen. And the fact that you have to go and live life in the normal world will be your punishment. Oh, I will be here and there and roundabout somewhere. I will be watching. I will be watching you fall to bits piece by piece, I will be watching you fall into tiny pieces of your former self and then I will be ready to pick up the pieces." Even I was having trouble working out Geena's plan now. But I was getting it slowly. "You see Tina you're not ready to come into the fold yet. Your journey isn't the same as Tara's. You have to be handled in a different way. But when you are ready, when 'I' think you are ready I will come for you. It's a simple thing. A really simple thing. But not yet. You haven't seen everything yet. I want you to see a little bit more before I get you dropped back home.

Chapter 15

I wished that Geena didn't have to be so cruel sometimes. I truly wished that. I knew all that she said, all that she taught me was right. Nothing she said was wrong and I was so grateful for everything because she was teaching me how girls like me had to live. I knew all of that. But she had told me that she had to be cruel to be kind. I guess I didn't know, or recognise the slow creeping and increasing cruelty that was there all the time. That was because I was becoming acclimatised to the way that I had to live and the way it had to be. I didn't realise that the whole way I was kept and treated by Geena was cruel. I didn't really realise that everything about it was cruel. That was because I was used to it. That was because I had become accustomed to the cruelty. It was when she stepped up the cruelty. When she turned up the cruelty - that was when it became stark and obvious. But I even knew that was necessary. I even knew that that cruelty was something that had to happen. I just wish that she had sent mum home before she did that this night. But she didn't. She wanted to teach mum as well. She wanted to show her how it had to be. It was like mum had to know and the only way she could know was to see it first-hand.

I knew that she had to be beyond cruel sometimes because that was the best way that I would learn that girls like me were different. I knew that. When she had put those things inside me, the things that vibrated the way they did to give me the beautiful never-ending orgasms, she had told me that it wouldn't always be about the pleasure. As screaming inside as I was sometimes for that orgasm to end, I didn't really mean that. Even when my legs had almost given way and I was shaking and desperate to go down sometimes, I never wanted to it end. I did and I didn't. It was one of

140

those weird things. I was stuck somewhere in the middle. But she had told me "You know Tara, sometimes it will be about the torture as well. Girl's like you need the pleasure. You need the orgasm but you also need to understand that you need the absolute hell as well. And as she had been telling me that I understood. I completely understood what she was saying.

I could have been all innocent and pretended that I didn't know or understand that I needed to suffer torture as well as that incessant pleasure. But I would have been lying. Of course I understood it. It stood to reason that it couldn't all be about that beautiful thing. And the way that Geena explained it to me, it made perfect sense. And it sounded perfectly plausible and normal that girls like me, that 'I' had to suffer the torture as well. It was like I had to pay for the way I was. For the kind of girl I was. One of those girls - whatever 'those girls' were.

That still didn't stop those flash thoughts from gushing through me though. The ones where I wished it didn't have to be like this. That thing she had put inside me, it could do both. Torture and pleasure. It could do them separately and it could do them both together. I don't know what it was that she had put inside me. She had been holding something and then she had slid all of her fingers, and this thing inside me and I had felt it settle in there. There was something strange about the way it felt. Almost as though it was alive in me. Almost as though it was organic. And that it was organically settling in inside me. Like it had found its nook and cranny inside me and was in there for the duration now. I didn't know what it was. I didn't even see what Geena had been holding before she slipped her fingers inside me. I didn't even know what it looked like. I just know what it felt like up inside me. I soon forgot it was there. That is until I questioned myself about how I could be feeling this amazing orgasm. Then I remembered it was

141

because of that. That it was helping me along. That it was that thing that was making the orgasm a never-ending thing.

That is, it was a never-ending thing until Geena changed it. Until she used her little remote-control thing and changed what that thing up inside me did. And that was what she did now that mum was here and watching. Then she started to play around with the remote. Started doing things with it. And started playing around with the little box of tricks that she had put up inside me. I didn't want her to play around with the orgasm though. I wanted that to go on and on and on. It must have been part of the mind fuck. When it was there, I had times when I wanted it to stop because it was so beautiful. But now I knew that Geena was going to play with me, now I knew that she was going to do things, and that the orgasm would be interrupted or stopped, I just wanted that to go on and on and on. I was prepared to have my mind fried if that orgasm could go on and on uninterrupted.

I howled when the orgasm was turned up. The drool from me catapulted out. And then it was stopped just stopped and I cried out again. Geena was playing with the remote control and she was doing something. Pressing buttons in a sequence to mix things up a bit. The orgasm stopped but there was something in its place. At first there was nothing in its place but then there was like a little tickle. A tickle that threatened that the orgasm would come back. That was what I wanted the most, for that orgasm to come back. But it didn't. Not straight away anyway. It just threatened and that altered the way I moved and stood on those boots. It altered my gate. It made me move in a way that I thought might make the orgasm come back. Of course, that couldn't happen. The orgasm could only come back if Geena allowed it to come back. If she made it come back. But she was in teaching mode again and she would only do what she had to do. She was teaching me and she was teaching mum. I was already on the long road to learning, but mum was only just starting.

"Your daughter is an 'addict' Tina. What you are seeing now is her addiction in full grip of her. This is what she is. It's not what she will become, it's what she is already. She is an addict. She is addicted to orgasm. She will do anything for an orgasm. It's what she lives for. A drug addict will live for their next fix. Always after the next buzz. Tara is like that except she lives for one thing and one thing alone. She lives for the orgasm. The orgasm that has to be used to control her." I had heard all of this before. It's what Geena had told me right at the start. It was what she had drummed into me and I believed every word of it. It all made sense to me, perfect sense. But mum was hearing it for the first time. I can't imagine what was going through her mind as Geena was explaining to her all about me. All about my addiction. I only had one addiction and that was right, the orgasm addiction. I wanted and needed that so bad that I cannot find words to describe it. But mum was hearing it for the first time.

It was funny really, not in a funny way. But I was aware of everything that Geena said despite what I was going through. I had to deal with what I was going through but at the same time I had glimpses of mum as she was taking in what Geena was saying. There was more than a little girl lost look about mum. I kind of understood that. She had been shocked I knew that. Mum won't have been shocked in this way ever. No matter what she did in the past to make ends meet, no matter what low life she had come across, nothing would have prepared her for this night. And that was showing on her face. She was unsteady on her high heels and mum was never but never unsteady on her high heels.

She was an 'expert' on her heels. She could wear the highest and the spikiest and be like she was born on them. But not in this red glowing room on his night. It was like she had had had a massive shock to her system, which of course she had. It was like that shock had slammed into her and then seeped through her pores and was on the way through her bodily systems. At one point it was like she was wavering. Like she was almost buckling at the knees. "She was never like that. You've made her like that. She was always a good girl. My good girl."

I could understand the way that mum was talking. It was all too much for her. Blame everybody except herself because of the shock. I got that. I understood that. She would understand eventually. I cried out again. Not because the orgasm was there again but because I wanted it to be. I needed it. It was like when Geena spoke about my addiction then it became ever more apparent to me. Like she was reminding me about it. Reminding me and letting me know that it was there and that it would always be there. And that thing up inside me was doing its bit to remind me as well. That tickling. The tickling would have been enough to bring the orgasm back, but it didn't. It was like there was something in the micro controller that prevented that final push into orgasm. It was like it was doing just enough to keep me on edge. Not on edge in the cold sense of the word. I remember that edging that Geena had started training me to. This was a different edge. One that was beyond maddening. I could only move so much what with the ankle chains and me being chained to the raised rubber platform. But my movements were more desperate. They were more erratic. They were more pronounced. And mum was looking at me with her head tilted slightly. Like she felt sorry for me or something. I guessed that she wished that she could

144

come and help me but she didn't make a move to do that. She just watched in a way that told me that she didn't know really what to do.

And I was dripping and for the first time I noticed mum really looking at me dripping from between the legs. In a way I wished that she wouldn't do that. I didn't want her to watch me. But that was me still learning. I would learn that anyone and everyone could watch me and see what I was and I had no rights to stop them, or to wish that they wouldn't watch me in that way. I could feel her eyes though, fixed and focused on the drips. It was like a slow motion. Me moving in the way that my addiction was forcing me to move, and then mum focussing on the drips that were falling from my extended sex lips to the rubber floor of the platform. And that was the other thing. Mum was focussing on my extended sex lips as well. I knew they had been extended and stretched and I knew that they would be visible to anyone who focussed down there. I wished mum hadn't done that though. I know now that I didn't have the right to wish that, and I don't now think like that. But that night it was part of the torture. The torture that I was going through. Mum seeing what I was, witnessing what I was in minute detail was part of the whole thing. It was part of the torment that I knew that I had to suffer. The slow motion of my own sex drips falling from my sex lips and my mother seeing that.

She had to learn though. She had to learn what I was and how it had to be. Then I cried out again. It was more like a screeching and a clenching of my thighs and knees together as the pain shot through me. I didn't know where exactly the pain was. It just felt like it was something that was infesting all of me. That pain. God that pain. Geena had done something with the remote control and that pain had come. It was like it had 'arrived'. But it didn't arrive in one place, it arrived right

145

through me. Everywhere through me. Even inside my head. I know it can't have really been like that but it just felt like it. It wasn't a localised pain, or one that I could pinpoint. It was just a general thing that affected all of me. A general thing but an acute thing as well.

I grunted and I moved in that latex cat an on those ballet heels in a different way yet again. Like I was trying to escape from the pain. I couldn't escape. Right when the pain was at its most acute I wanted the orgasm back more than ever. I needed it to be back. Of course, I would learn in time that the pain and the other stuff that Geena did to me was designed to make me more addicted to the orgasm. If I was given severe pain, then I would crave the pleasure to be back. It was like something that Geena was doing, and would do over time. Her work with me would never be done in that respect. Simple addiction was not enough for her to inflict me with. It had to be absolute soul destroying addiction that was vital at all costs.

"Please don't hurt her like that, please stop hurting her?" I'd never heard mum cower and plead with anyone before. Mum wasn't like that. She had never been like that. It was like she had been through her share of hard times and she wouldn't be cowed by anyone. But that wasn't the case here. She was pleading with Geena to stop the hurt flowing through me. Although I wanted the pain to stop, I knew that I had to suffer it. I don't even know why I had to suffer it. If I really think about it. What did I ever do to anyone to deserve it? I might have been different to other girls, god knows, Geena had told me that enough times, but I didn't quite get how I had to suffer like this. Or maybe I did. I didn't know much of anything anymore. Just that I had to get through this so the orgasm could come back. In a way if I could just settle into the torture, just ride it through and get over it knowing that the orgasm would be back soon enough, then it would be ok. It would all be ok again.

It might have been easier if I could have used my hands or my arms to hold across my tummy to ease that pain a little bit. Not that it would have. But I couldn't do that. I wasn't allowed. Just like I wasn't allowed to touch myself down there to assist the pleasure that Geena was letting me have at any given time. I couldn't touch myself or assist myself in any way. That was a strict no no. "She needs the hurt Tina. Your little girl needs the hurt so that her addiction is better for her." I guess to anyone normal none of this would make any sense. It wouldn't make any sense at all. In fact, I am sure it would sound ludicrous. It would have sounded so to mum. But she wasn't quite as normal as she had been earlier this same night.

She was being eased into Geena's world. But that didn't stop the bemused look she had on her face. She was trying to work out why it was a good idea for her little girl to be in such absolute pain. And she would have known that I was in that pain. She would have known that I was in some kind of dire pain. She would have known that I was in so much pain that I would have done anything to make it stop. But then I would have done anything to let that orgasm be back as well. That was what I needed. For that orgasm to come back. For that pain to fade away and that orgasm to come back.

Then the tickle was back. That maddening tickle. The pain stopped and the tickle was back. And with that tickle came more of a dripping from my sex lips. I grunted and then I groaned. At least that pain had stopped. Maybe the next time Geena played with that remote control she would give me the orgasm back. I'd be so grateful to her if she did that. I would be so grateful to her if she let me have that pleasure back. I kind of understood that this treatment was what she needed to give to me. I understood that this was what I had to experience. That I had to get used to. But I understood the cruelty involved as well. I didn't get completely why Geena had to be so cruel in order to be kind. But then I did as well. She would explain things to me and I would get it then. That was what she did so well. When I didn't understand something, like why I couldn't go home to be with my mum in our normal world, she would take time out and explain it all and then it would all make sense. The way she explained things and the way she made me understand. It was like a gentle but complete coercion into her way of thinking. Into her way of life really.

Now it was pure sexual noises that I was making. Because the sight, or the sense of that orgasm was there again. It was within touching distance - but just not there yet. It was still just out of touching distance. But I was moving more fluidly again. Moving on those heels more suggestively, swaying the hips a little more provocatively. And the drips from down between my legs were thicker. Like the real sex juice was coming out now. It was thicker. The drips got heavier on my sex lips before gravity won over and made them let go. I looked down at the rubber floor of the platform and it was splattered with my juices. In places there were puddles. In a way it was easy to map my movements from the puddles of sex juice on the floor. And then it came again. Then the orgasm came again.

Chapter 16

Oh fuck, that orgasm. That beautiful orgasm. It came again. But it was different this time. There was more to it. There was more substance to it. It was a 'thicker' orgasm. Just like my juices were thicker, so to was the orgasm. That is the only way that I can describe it. A thicker more substantial orgasm. And because it was thicker, it was more intense. I never thought my orgasmic state could be topped but it was each and every time. Each and every time it was topped and then topped again. And this time my eyes rolled such was its effect. It felt as though that thing inside me had come fully to life and it was making itself more and more beautiful. One of my long-rubbered legs buckled. I felt it, but then it snapped back into place. The chains rattled. Fuck! My pussy, inside my pussy was tightening and squeezing. It was like it had a life of its own and was determined to get the most pleasure out of that thing inside me. Like it was sucking the pleasure out of it.

And then I was dripping. I couldn't work out how I was producing so much sexual drool. And it was sexual drool. Pure drool was pouring from me as I was having this orgasm. This beautiful orgasm. And then it seemed when that orgasm was at its height, just when it couldn't get any more intense it stopped. She took it off me. Geena took it off me. And it was around this time that I wished that the pain would come back. Because if the pain came back then I would have something to take my mind off the orgasm that has been taken off me. But the pain didn't come back. There was just 'nothing'. Absolutely nothing. It was like I couldn't feel anything inside me. Nothing at all. How could she do that? How could Geena and that thing inside me make me feel 'nothing'. I made another sound, like a sound of frustrated distress. That was because I was frustrated and

I was in distress. How could that orgasm just be 'gone'? How could it be just not there anymore? How could something so huge, so magnificent, so beautiful be there one second and gone the next? I couldn't get my head round that, I just couldn't. There was nothing. And my sounds, the sounds of frustration and distress were compounded and joined by my sobs and the little stomps of my ballet heeled feet.

I wanted that orgasm back so badly that I sobbed. And that was the torture. Me not having an orgasm. But not just me not having that orgasm, but having nothing. Like this big whole 'nothing' in its place. That made the addiction more acute. It was like some kind of spell had been broken. That the orgasm and its effects were the spell and somehow this had been broken and the whole thing had just vanished. And all that was left was me. A wanting needing absolutely distraught me. And that was another word, distraught. I was on that raised platform, chained to it and with my steps impeded by another chain. But I had to cope with that. I had to just stay there in front of my mother and deal with it. But I wasn't dealing with it. I needed to have that dripping drenching orgasm back. I just needed it and because I didn't have it, I just sobbed and sobbed. "What's the matter with her, why is she sobbing like that? What have you done to her now?" And mum' sounded as bemused as she looked. She didn't know the orgasm had been taken off me. How could she? All she knew was that I was in this pleasure one second and then something changed. She didn't know that the orgasm had just been taken away, had just been stopped.

"I've taken the orgasm away. She needs orgasm so bad Tina. So bad she needs that pleasure and when she doesn't have it, when she doesn't get it, this is what happens. What you see now is your little girl in withdrawal. What you are seeing now is a girl so needy,

150

so wanting of that orgasm to be back that she will do more than anything to get it back. A little later, before you go - before I let you go home to your normal life I will show you that she will do anything just to get that pleasure back." I could hear the conversation. I could hear it as though it was being fed electronically into my ears. Crystal clear. Geena told me that my senses would become more heightened. And that they would become more acute. And that was certainly the case. "Please, please just give it back to her. Let her have it back, please Geena. I don't like seeing her like this. Please give it back to her." There it was again, mum pleading. Something that she never did. It sounded weird to me. It sounded as though mum shouldn't have been pleading like that, even if she was doing it on my behalf. I shared her sentiment. I really did, I wanted that orgasm back so badly that I would certainly have done anything. Absolutely anything.

"Oh no Tina, not just yet. I want you to see what the effects of Tara not having that orgasm are. I want you to see it and witness it." I have to admit that Geena's words often chilled me to the bone. And the way she was when she spoke like this chilled me. Her voice, the way she used the words, the tone she used. It was like her own deepest fantasies were being realised in what she was doing to me. Like she was lost in the moment herself. I was hearing the words, every single one of them. And then I had to process them. I am thinking now that this was Geena upping the cruelty level. She had been coercing me into her world up to now. She had just been gently taking me into her world. But now that she knew I was there, now that she knew that there was no going back for me, she was upping the cruelty. And that was a fact. There was no going back for me. It had been Geena's intention to inflict me with this addiction and this is what she had done. And there must have come a point when she realised that she had done this. It must have been clear to her before now. But now she was certain that there would be no climbing out of that addiction for me. Now she knew it was a permanent fixture of my character. An orgasm addicted 'thing'.

It was funny really that that was what I was considering myself. When there was nothing there, when that orgasm was somewhere else, a long way away from me, I was thinking that I was just a thing. I didn't feel like I was Tara at all. That was my mind working overtime. That was what it did when it had nothing else to occupy it. If the orgasm was there I would be busy in the mind conjuring up filthy images to feed the orgasm. But there was none of that and because my mind refused to be redundant, it got thinking in other ways. It got thinking in ways maybe that were not good for me as a whole.

Or not good for me when taking the bigger picture into consideration. I was putting myself down. I was accepting what I was, what Geena had spent time, intense time telling me I was, teaching me what I was, and now I was furthering that teaching of me. Furthering that rewiring of my mind and brain. I had gone from scream inducing pain, through the incessant teases of the tickles, through to the knee weakening orgasm and then to nothing. All that was left was what mum and Geena could see on the raised platform. I felt wrecked - more than wrecked.

"You want it back don't you Tara? You want the orgasm back?" She was deliberately not saying that I needed that orgasm back. She was avoiding that because she wanted me to come out with it, as though it was some kind of earth shattering confession I was going to make. But in reality she knew that it would indeed be earth shattering for mum to hear me say this. For me to admit it, confess it. "Yes, yes please yes. Please can I have it back? I need it Geena I NEED it. Please, please can I have it, please?" And there it was. The begging pleading and the confession that I needed the centre of my sexuality to be exploding in orgasm. I needed that back. I looked at mum through my own despair and I could see her's deepening. I was thinking that it wasn't so bad mum. I could have been confessing to being a cocaine addict or something. She would understand that. I knew that she did cocaine from time to time and had done for years. I could have been confession to being a crack whore. But I wasn't. I was just addicted to orgasm - the beautiful thing. Was that such a bad thing? I didn't think so. But then my mind was hardly wired up right at this time.

I could feel the eyes on me. Mum's eyes and Geena's. In a way this step was as new to Geena as it was to mum. Geena was taking me further than she had before and this was a huge step. Taking away any sense of pleasure. Removing any sensation of pleasure. Having installed that addiction and then removing the source of that pleasure and just leaving me in that raised platform in my rubber and intense heels to cope with that. And that was the thing. That was something that was striking me - the rubber. It became like my friend. I don't know how to explain that or describe it. There was no orgasm and I was rocking on my heels because of that. But the skin-tight fit of the latex, and the sheer height of the heels that I had on were like things that brought me closer to orgasm. They had been the things that had helped me become what Geena wanted me to become. And although the orgasm wasn't there now, I could feel the rubber clinging to me. The smell and the aroma was back. I suppose I was trying to replace the orgasm with something. And because the rubber and the high heels were sexual in orientation, because everything was sexual to me - those heels and the way they made me

153

stand, and walk and move, I guess deep down, deep deep down I was hoping upon hope that Geena's cruelty wouldn't stretch to removing the rubber and the heels.

But no - the rubber room, my cell, and the spiked ballet heels that seemed to be a part of me now, were my one string to that orgasm. She wouldn't move those. She would never be sure of the effect of removing the rubber and the heels. Especially when she was watching, and studying the effects on me of having removed the orgasm. I was aware, as aware as I was desperate of moving suggestively again - trying to rekindle that sexuality in me. As though if I moved and stepped sexily then the orgasm might come back. It was the desperation that I was in. It was the sheer need in me to feel that orgasm rock my world again. "Look for fucks sakes Geena give it to her back. You can see the state she is in." That was my mum. She wasn't begging and pleading and cowing to Geena now. It was like she had got over that and was just angry at seeing me suffer like this. I loved my mother. I had forgotten it but I knew it again at this point. But when I think now, that was the selfish in me. That was me loving her because she was trying to get me back what I needed so much. It sounded like the old mum. If she had to raise her voice then she would, but she wouldn't do that very often. It made it more effective when she did raise her voice. Except that none of that had any effect on Geena. This was Geena's world.

Geena smiled. "You want her to have it back as much as she wants it herself don't you Tina? I wonder. I just wonder what you would do to let her have it back. What would you be willing to do, just so that Tara can be in that euphoria of orgasm again?" And in her few words she had turned things on her head. She had completely twisted things round. She had put the pressure onto mum. She had shocked me in what she had said. Nothing inside my mind would have even hinted at

154

pressure being put onto mum because of what I needed and what I wanted so badly.

And yet this was it. It was like a moment in time. Like a snapshot in time. It was as though the moment had been frozen. Geena had asked the question and there was this silence. Even in that split second my despair was forgotten. I was as interested in what mum would say or do in response as Geena must have been. Geena was clever like that - she knew how to take situations, and people and use them to her own benefit. I hadn't worked it out then, but I have now. It wasn't enough that she had me where she wanted me. It wasn't enough that I was this tormented soul on extreme heels, shrink wrapped in latex and willing to do anything, absolutely anything in order to feel that orgasm again. She wanted more. She always wanted more. I know now that Geena was a sadist. She was a pure, undiluted sadist and she would never be satisfied with what she had achieved. She would always want more and need more. She would always be looking for the next big buzz. And it was like she had found just that. It was like she had found the next big buzz in mum.

Mum didn't answer straight away. It was like she was as much caught up in that 'moment' as I was. It must have been like a shock question for her to have to answer. Like what was she supposed to say? What was she supposed to answer to that question? I guessed that she could only answer the way any mother would answer. "Ok, ok, ok. Look I'll do anything. Just give it to her back please, now. I'll do anything. Look take me instead, let her go, and take me instead. I'll do anything. I promise you." And that was the thing, mum didn't give it to Geena in dribs and drabs, she didn't hesitate in what she was saying. She gave it all in one go. Like she didn't want to mince her words. Like she didn't want there to be any misunderstanding - she just wanted to put herself out there. Geena smiled and then she laughed softly.

"Oh Tina that is sweet. You know, you may regret putting yourself on the rack like that. I know that Rob dearly, dearly wants to have some fun with you and believe me when I say that his idea of fun will not be the same as yours. As for you taking the place of Tara - that is a sweet idea as well but not one that will happen this side of hell freezing over. But you know, you have got me thinking. You have got me thinking how I can use your 'offer' to progress matters. I am all for progress. And I hadn't figured you into the proceedings to any great degree, other than to ensure you stayed in your place. But now I think about it. I'm in the process of destroying your little girl and I don't see any problems with destroying mum as well. In fact, I quite like the idea. Like a double destruction - like a cataclysmic double destruction of mum and offspring."

I didn't like the way that Geena was talking. She was using that tone again. A tone that said that she was in some kind of 'zone'. She was using that tone more and more lately. It was like she had broken free from the mundane and was back where she wanted to be herself. Where she needed to be. I was still in shock from hearing mum offering herself. I have to say I was so desperate for the orgasm to be back that I didn't care if Geena had taken her up on the offer of exchanging me for her. Just as long as I could have that gorgeous beautiful orgasm back again. I would have gladly, willingly watched mum be taken into the abyss if I could have felt that thing back again. That thing, that orgasm inside me just possessing me.

But then there was the other stuff that Geena was saying. About destroying me and destroying mum. That really scared me. In the bigger scheme of things, I still needed that orgasm back and nothing would take that

156

need away from me. But what Geena was saying was nagging at the back of my mind. She had been the one helping me, helping me to be what I needed to be, what I had been all the time but didn't know. She was the one who was helping me be what I had to be. The one who would help me live like I needed to live. But now she was using words like 'destroy', 'destruction' and 'destroying'. Her tone had changed. The words she was using had changed and everything had changed.

I was kind of blaming mum for that change. For telling Geena that she would do anything and that she would swap places. It had been alright, it had been fine until mum was brought here and now she had done this. This is how fucked up my mind had become. Correction this was how fucked up Geena had made my mind be. I couldn't see it then. I can see it now but it's too late now. It was too late then as well if truth be known. Geena didn't say anything else for a long time. I was in the despair and the need of wanting that orgasm back, mum was in this state of utter shock and bemusement by what she had seen and what she had heard since she met Geena. And there was just this silence. I was making little noises as I moved as much as the chains would allow me to. I wished someone would say something.

I just wished that something, anything would happen. I was dripping. But I was dripping because I was trying to squeeze myself round that thing inside me - that was my body taking over, trying to get that orgasm back. My body doing its own thing as I dripped and as I sobbed. I tried to stop sobbing, and that worked. But it only worked to a point and then the sobbing came back. It was like some kind of crossroads had been reached. Like an impasse. I didn't care about the impasse. I could have stayed with the impasse if I was in that orgasmic state. But I wasn't, and that was wearing me down more and more.

Chapter 17

"You see Tina, words are easy. Words are just so easy to pour off the tongue. Your words offering yourself. Tara's words telling me that she would do anything, absolutely anything so that she could have that orgasm back. But you know, the proof of the pudding is in the eating." She was using that tone again but she had upped it a little bit more. I didn't know what she was going to say next. The truth be known I didn't give a flying fuck. I wasn't afraid to show that I would do anything, absolutely anything in order to get that orgasm back. That wasn't something I just said. I meant it. I meant every word of it, but I meant it from the bottom of my soul as well.

But then there was that other thing. The proof of the pudding is in the eating - that was what she said. I could prove my bit. That meant she would want mum to prove her part as well. That didn't settle right on my psyche. It didn't settle well at all. It didn't matter that I was gripped with the addiction. And I was 'gripped'. She was still my mum. She was still the one whom had given birth to me. It still mattered. I didn't think it would, but it did. I wanted that orgasm more than ever now. If I had that I wouldn't have to think about mum and what she might have to do for me. But it was catch 22. Here I was without orgasm and here was Geena with me willing to do anything and mum also willing to do anything. It was win win for her. More than win win. Yes, I was still craving from the core of my femininity for the orgasm to be back, but I was still more than aware, hyper-aware actually, of everything that was happening around me. I wished this wasn't the case. Even now I wished I hadn't been aware of what was happening in the red glowing rubber room that night.

The longer I went without orgasm, the more broken down I felt. The more broken down I became. I didn't think I would be able to identify that, but I could. It was like I was a witness, step by step to my own breaking down. That was odd that was. It was all part of my own demolishing. The heightened senses and the being aware of every little tiny thing that was to do with me. It wasn't like that in orgasm. I could just immerse in orgasm and although the senses remained heightened, I could just immerse to a point that I didn't care. That was because I didn't care. That was the selfish addict in me. But somehow, as I stood on that raised platform, my debilitated steps becoming more and more awkward, I had a feeling that there would have been more to it than mum just sucking Rob the mute's cock. I should have been repulsed by that sight. My own mother with a thick cock pistoning in and out of her mouth.

But the fact was that I wasn't repulsed. I was jealous. Such was my neediness, such was my need for orgasm to be back, such was my thinking that 'I' was at the centre of the sexual world, that I was also thinking that mum had no right to be sucking that cock right now. That should have been my job, because I was the one that Geena had taken in. If anyone should have sucked that cock, then it should have been me. In my mind it was all pretty straight. In my mind there was nothing to discuss or straighten out. Mum had no right to be sucking that cock, even if she was doing it for me. And the thing was that she was doing it for me. She was sucking that cock as part of the deal that would, or should get me into the state of orgasm again. I was watching her through my own despair and my own need. Her thick red lips wrapped and sealed round that cock head. She made me sick. Not because she was sucking that cock, but because of how good at it she was.

It was all coming true now - it was all there for me to see. All that I had heard in the past about what mum had done to make a living through the years. We had never talked about that in the starkest terms. It was like one of those things that was never talked about. It was never even alluded to. It might have been something that had taken place and something that had happened, but it wasn't something that was talked about. And yet here it was now, the proof as it were - the proof that mum used to suck cocks for a living. That proof being in how good at it she was. How competent that she was at pleasuring a cock with her mouth. That was what made me sick. I could have done just as good a job as that. I could have used my mouth in the same way as her and brought Rob the mute off. But it was her. And this is how fucked up it was - she was doing it for me and yet I was jealous that she was doing at all. It should have been me. I was so needing the orgasm back that I wanted to suck cock just because it was sexual. A dirty sexual thing.

I still had that feeling though. I still had that nagging feeling that it wouldn't be enough. Even as Rob was offloading inside mum's mouth - even as he was emptying his balls inside her mouth and down her throat I had a feeling that it wouldn't be the end of it. That that wouldn't be all that she would have to do. If it was, then I could watch her swallow that cum and then get myself all ready for the return of my orgasm. But I had more than a strong feeling that that wouldn't be the case. I had a feeling that there would be much more to it than that. In a way, as well as being jealous of mum, I had this envy as well. Rob was a copious cummer. I knew that. I had had to pleasure him so I knew. He wasn't just 'big', he was a copious cummer and mum had taken it all in her stride. She had wrapped her lips and her whole mouth round that cock as though she didn't want any of that delicious cum to escape and then she had sucked

160

him dry. And there had been that movement in her throat, like a rolling swallow that told that she was taking it all down inside her. Fucking bitch, that was my cum! But it wasn't over for her, not yet.

There was a spell, an amount of time that passed between mum swallowing Rob's cum and what happened next, when my despair was at its height. When it was at its most acute. I think whilst I could focus through the wall of need and despair, on my mum sucking and pleasuring that cock, I could just about push the need for that orgasm to the back of my mind. Not out of my mind, but just push it back a little bit. It would have been impossible to push it out of my mind totally, the need and the addiction was just too much, too strong for that. But then she was taken from in front of me to the side, to one corner of the red glowing room. A little spot light was turned on and there was a chair. A heavy wooden chair that was fixed to the rubber floor of the room. That chair was on a raised platform as well. I knew all about that chair. I had been on it. I guess it was about this time that I should have been really worried about mum. I should have been worried about her because I knew the kind of things that happened in that corner of the room on that chair.

The fact was I wasn't worried about her. My addiction, and my low because I was not receiving orgasm was at its most acute. I understood drug addiction because addicts got medically addicted. The drugs did things to their systems to make them addicted. To an extent I understood my addiction to orgasm. I understood that I needed it but not why. I hadn't taken drugs to alter my immune system. Yes, I had been given extreme, extreme intense pleasure that had melted my mind and I wanted and needed that back. But I didn't understand how I could be addicted the way I was. I didn't understand how or why I was feeling like the world would end if I didn't get that orgasm again soon. It must have been all in my mind. Indeed, I know that it was psychological now. I didn't know then. Maybe I wasn't supposed to know then. All I did know was that there was this screaming in my head for the pleasure to be back and that if it was back it would all be ok. It was the equivalent of the crack whore craving her next fix. I too was craving my next fix. I needed it, I needed it badly but it wasn't coming.

Even through the strongest and most needy cravings I had experienced to date I was aware of Geena and Rob preparing mum for the next phase. I was having my feelings confirmed, that it wouldn't be quite as simple as a cock suck for Geena to be satisfied that mum had done 'anything' so that I could have that orgasm back again. I was aware of Geena down, taking off the chains. Yes she was taking off the chains. I wasn't sure what that meant. But then I was having trouble thinking straight. I was aware of everything but thinking straight was not included in the deal. She was taking chains off, releasing me. Allowing me to move more freely. But then she was taking my hand and she was leading me off the raised platform. That was an odd feeling. Being so long with those ankle chains on - being so long being anchored to that raised platform. And then to have my long legs free again it felt odd. Like for just a little while I kept my steps little ones, little hobbled steps, in case I had got it all wrong. And then the strides, the long strides only coming back very eventually. I was being led to another corner. The corner opposite mum.

If I could have chosen not to watch what was happening to mum then I would have taken that option. My addiction and my craving had reached new levels, and yet there was something left in me that told me that I shouldn't watch what they did next. As it was I had had to watch them lower her down so that she was sitting on the upturned phallic things. Two of them. One for her ass and one for her pussy. Mum being helped up onto the step, then helped to sit, and then made to lower herself down onto this upturned dildo. I watched her take them. The whole length and thickness of them inside her. I watched her absorb them. There was a worry for her. But that worry was masked and it was filtered by my own addiction. And then there was the fact that I was jealous again. She was getting the attention down there between her legs. At least she had that. I didn't have that. I wasn't even allowed to touch myself. If I could touch myself I could bring myself to my own orgasm. The next best thing would be to have obscene looking phallic things slipped up inside me, but I didn't have that, mum had that. Bitch! She was having it all and I was having nothing.

My chair didn't have upturned phallic objects waiting to invade my femininity. Oh, there were holes for them to be there. It was an identical heavy wooden chair to the one that mum had sat on. Except that I just sat on the flat seat of the chair, my pussy lips squelching outside of the rubber. Me sliding round in my own juices. Because yes, those juices still came. Those juices still squeezed and oozed out of me. That was my addiction just helping to produce ooze after ooze of those juices. But no phallic objects. Just me be being helped onto the chair and sat down. I'm not sure if I was even curious as to what came next. I remember sitting on the chair and the pressure of me sitting on my pussy just making the need and the craving more so. But I'm not sure that I knew what I was sitting there for. The first thing I became consciously aware of next were the screams of mum. That was odd for me. That kind of dragged me out of this dire shit that I was in for micro split seconds. Mum's screams - and they were screams. I hadn't even seen mum cry let alone scream. Oh, we had

163

been reduced to tears of laughter before in the past. That was a regular thing. But I had never seen or heard her like this.

This wasn't regular this screaming. And it was a blood curdling screaming. With the first of the series of screams I held my breath because the sound was so piercing. It was so shocking. Geena and Rob weren't doing anything to her. What was happening to her was inside her. Those phallic things up inside her were causing her to scream like that. That was because they were being inflated inside her. They were already big when they slipped up into her. But once she had been settled on that chair - once the full weight of her was on them, they were made bigger. They were inflated. Made thicker and longer. And that was what was causing the screams. With every little incremental increase in size of the two dildos mum was spasming and cramping down there and it was really, really hurting her. And even as they were inflating inside her, Geena was securing her ankles. She was pulling her feet off the rubber floor and she was suspending them behind her so that her full weight was on those dildos inside her. And that inflation was something that was carried out on auto. A little bit at a time. One cramp at a time. One spasm at a time. Once ear piercing scream at a time.

"This is what you call 'doing anything for your little girl' Tina. I knew you could do it. And now I am just wondering how much you can take of this. This is what I want to know. How much of this you can take. You know, things like these dildos inside you are usually made with a safety device fitted in. A little trick that stops them being inflated beyond dangerous levels. But these ones have had the trickery taken out of them. They can just be inflated and inflated and inflated. There is no limit to how much they can be enlarged. And added to that is that there is no flesh that can stop them inflating.

164

The flesh will give. It will break down and it will tear. That flesh up inside you, ruined. So, I am wondering, just wondering how much of this you can take. I guess we are going to find out. We're going to find out how much you can take before its Tara's turn to impress me. And all because she wants and needs orgasm. You see the price of addiction Tina. It affects everyone. Everyone has to pay. Not just the addict, but everyone. Everyone pays in the end."

There it was again, that tone of voice that Geena was using. The one that told me she was in her own little zone. I didn't like that, it unsettled me. Made me feel unsettled inside. There was a conflict in me - how I could be existing in this state of addictive need, how I could be simply craving this pleasure to be back at the same time as my own mother was suffering the way she was.? And that was the thing, she was suffering. I could tell she was in this acute pain from the look of horror and from the expression on her face. I hadn't seen mum look like that before. It could have been that I would have been confused by how she was looking. That terror in her eyes, the looks of sheer fright and pain that she was feeling. But there was no mistake. I knew that she was suffering to her very core. I wanted and needed that pleasure and I would have killed for it. Right at that very moment I would have still killed for the orgasm to be back before I went to help my own mother. And there she was, sitting on that chair, with all her weight on those two expanding dildos inside her, suffering for me just so that I could have that orgasm. At least that was the plan but it was by no means assured or guaranteed. I'll let you into a little secret - if I had been given a gun and told the only way I would get the orgasm back is to shoot your mother in the head, then I would have. I would have done that without thinking twice about it.

"Area you watching Tara? Are you watching your mum suffering for you?" There was more than a little mocking in the tone that Geena used. "I'm not sure that she can suffer enough to warrant giving you an orgasm though. Let's wait and see, shall we?" And yet more mocking. Geena was letting both me and mum know that it was her that controlled things and decided things and made decisions about things. That it wasn't mum who decided she would suffer so that I could have an orgasm. But that it was her who decided if mum could suffer enough for me to deserve to be back in that orgasmic state. It was cruelty extended. It was cruelty off the scale. It was Geena showing the kind of woman she really was. Even I was seeing another side of Geena that I hadn't seen before. Even I was sensing her darkest side. Or was it just that it was all becoming clear to me now?

Maybe I should have begged her to stop that expansion of those dildos in mum. Yes, maybe I should have. But not at the expense of losing the chance of being given the intense pleasure again. That was what addiction had done to me. Maybe this was what Geena had meant when she said she was going to 'ruin' me. Maybe I was already ruined. What daughter wouldn't save their mum from this kind of torture? What daughter wouldn't force herself out of that addiction in order that her mum wouldn't feel like she was being ripped apart from the inside out? Obviously I didn't care enough to stop it.

All I was thinking about was the purest of pleasure that would be given to me if I was lucky. I could only prey to one god or another that what mum was suffering and then what I would have to do to prove myself, was enough. Mum let out another blood curdling scream and she seemed to shift on the seat. But that made it worse. That made the pain inside her worse. And it made her expressions more shocking. There was this gaunt look to

166

mum's face as those things grew inside her again. She nibbled her bottom lip. I got the impression that she was trying not to show me how much she was hurting. But that wasn't working - I just knew that she was in an agony that she wouldn't be able to put into words. If I was to ask her to describe the pain she was in to me she wouldn't be able to.

Chapter 18

Mum was in a constant state of tremble on that chair. That was because she was in a constant state of acute and abominable pain. Her face was a mixture of a mask of pain, of absolute agony and her trying to hide it. It was like despite what she was going through inside her, inside her femininity she didn't want to break down in front of me. Anything but that. But she was too far gone to realise that she had already broken down. She already looked and sounded wretched. But Geena wasn't happy with that. There had to be more that she could do, just to turn that scream up a little bit more. And there was. She had moved behind her, unsecured her ankles and then secured them just a little higher up behind her. She secured her ankles to her thighs and to the chair that she was sitting on. Maximum weight through the core of her spine and down through those phallic things inside her. There was this shriek. It was like a shriek of disbelief from mum. Like she couldn't believe that Geena had wanted to hurt her more and then went and did it.

I sat and watched. I don't know what I felt. It was like I was dead inside watching mum suffer like that. I knew what I should have felt but all I did actually feel was that I needed that orgasm more and more. I felt, like shit really that seeing mum suffer like this didn't stop me wanting that orgasmic state to be back. But the fact was that it didn't. If anything, I was working out that the more that mum suffered, the more likely that I was to be granted my wish. The more I was likely to be put into euphoria again. It was weird that I was thinking like that and at the same time knowing it was wrong. But I can't lie. It was how it was. I did try to imagine how mum felt. And what she was feeling at this precise time. I wished I wasn't trying to imagine because I didn't like what my mind and my imagination was coming up with. I just didn't. That was the thing about my state of being. My imagination, in order to feed the orgasmic state was capable of imagination things that it shouldn't have. It was weird that. The way the mind comes up with more and more extremes in sexuality the more extreme the state of being. And all just to feed my addictive and selfish need.

Then Geena worked on mum's some more. She took her hands and her arms behind her and she secured them. Even in my state of mind I winced at how she secured her arms. A tight latex band around her elbows. Just above the joints. And that then brought her elbows together. All the way together until they were touching. Mum was screaming with her breasts thrust forward, almost tipping out of the dress. She was making this sound first, like a wet sound from the back of her throat and then there was this almighty scream. A series of sounds and a series of screams. Those screams soul destroying. Mum's elbows touching and then her wrists being brought together in reverse prayer. There were those wet sounds and those screams but there were also the grunts. Deep guttural grunts that came from mum. I thought at this point that enough was enough. But it wasn't. Her wrists then suspended behind her, out straight. All of this bondage creating intense pressure on the spine but also intense pressure on the inflatable dildos inside her. And then with a smile Geena set about letting those dildos inflate just a little bit more. Just a series of little hisses as incremental increases in size of thickness and length was applied to the dildos.

And that was the time when mum really screamed. Like she screamed as though she didn't give a flying fuck who saw her or who heard her. She was still screaming when Geena turned to me. I had seen Geena in many states, in many 'moods' and with many expressions on her face. I couldn't understand then that what I was seeing at this point was a woman who was at the height of her sadistic state. There was this smile on her face, like an enigmatic smile that chilled me. I didn't know why it chilled me the way it did. It just did! "And so I come to you sweet Tara. What are you going to do for me? What are you going to do to prove that the need to have the orgasm so badly? I want to see now that the pressure is on you, what you can do for me. And in what you can do for me, what you can do for yourself?" My eyes were flicking back and for from Geena to mum and back again - and that on repeat. It was difficult for me to think because of the din that mum was making.

I suspected that that it was hard for me to think, that it was hard for me to make sense of any of this, was a deliberate thing. That it was part of this world that Geena had made. Part of the world that she had created. It wasn't all about the physical pain. It was about the psychological pressure and that mental hurt. "What, what do you want me to do Geena. I'll do anything. You know that. You know I'll do anything to feel that niceness come back into my body. You know that." I was trying to mask that I was caring about my mum. I was split in two. I needed that pleasure - of course I did. But seeing mum suffering like this was having an effect on my psyche. It wasn't to the point that I was prepared to save her and not have the orgasmic state back. And that was what was tearing me apart. That was what the torture was for me. It was a two-level torture - the being denied the orgasm and seeing my mum in the way she was suffering. That had to be having a longer-term effect on me. I didn't realise it at the time but I do now.

The sound of mum in agony seemed to pierce every other sound that was happening. Geena was timing her little sentences, between the din of those screams. She had gone to the side of the room and then come back carrying something. A little velvet case. It looked like a case that could have held an expensive item of jewellery. Maybe a neckless or a bracelet. But somehow, I knew that this wasn't what it was. Geena was smiling. She was smiling because she knew what was in the case and what she wanted me to do. I had had no warning or no clue as to what she was going to say or what she was going to get me to do. She came in front of me and there was this little shudder down the core of my spine. With what I had been through, I didn't know why I had that feeling down my spine. Or maybe I do. I don't know. Geena got down on her heels and she used my own knees to balance then she opened the case. She did it in a way that I was bound to look. I was bound to look down and see what was in the case.

I looked at the stainless steel, and I looked at the ultra-sharp points. It was like I spent a long time looking at what was in the case. Long needles with points that looked lethal. Lethal points that tapered to nothingness and yet which told at the same time that they would push through flesh with the ease of a red-hot needle through a slap of semi frozen butter. Those needles looked lethal and they looked frightening. The taper of each very gradual and into the thickness where at the end at which they would be held, they were thick, rubberised. Those needles were made and designed to be handled. They were designed to be handled and pushed through flesh. There was no doubt about that. I just looked. I looked at the open case, I looked at the full, complete set of needles and then I looked back at Geena.

"Pick one out Tara. Any one of them. Pick it out and hold it. Feeling it between your thumb and forefinger. I want you to get the feel for it." Geena was talking in that tone of voice again. She was talking from her zone. I don't know what it was about the way she spoke - that word always came back to me, that she was in her own 'zone'. It was a word that would stay with me. It would always stay with me. I didn't know which needle to take out of the case. It was a set of ten. Needles from a small size to a large size. Needles that just told me that it didn't matter which one I chose, that the damage that they could do to flesh would simply be lesser or more. I didn't want to choose the larger or the smaller because for some fucked up reason in my mind that would show a preference. So, I went straight down the middle. I chose the middle-sized needle just easing it out of the case and holding it by the thumb grip. Another shudder when down my spine but this time it was down the outside of my spine as I held up the needle. Easily six inches in length and that taper from a nothing point to the thickness of the thumb grip so gradual and so frightening to see up close.

"How does it feel hmm? How does it feel to roll that between your thumb and forefinger?" It was weird again. I was doing exactly that, rolling the needle between my thumb and forefinger. "Feels nice." I was lying. I just thought that would be what Geena would want to hear. At this point I had no idea what she would want me to do, or what I would have to do with the selected needle. "That's right. It feels 'nice'. Do you have any idea what I want you to do with it. Hmm?" And Geena was still smiling. Of course I didn't know. I just moved my head side to side in the negative. As I did that I was squeezing my intimate inner flesh around that thing that was inside me. I had a feeling that Geena would want me to stroll right on over to mum and begin torturing her with the needle that I had selected from the velvet case. She had released me from the chains that had been holding me on the raised platform and she had sat me down so that I could see the things she did to mum. It stood to reason that she would make me torture mum now - that I would

172

have to hurt her more than she was hurting already with this lethal needle that I had selected.

But once again I was wrong. And Geena had this smile on her face which told me that she knew that I was thinking all of the wrong things. "We'll wait until mum settles down Tara. Wait until she had absorbed all of that pain inside her and until she is focusing what is happening around her, and then I want you to take the needle you have chosen and push it through the base of each of your nipple. I want you to make sure mum sees you doing this to yourself. I want you to make sure she takes it all in." I was hearing the words that she was speaking but at first I couldn't comprehend them. I had been waiting for her to tell me to go hurt my own mum. On first thoughts that would have been the worst thing that she could have told me to do. To tell a needy, dripping girl to go hurt her mother so that she had can have more pleasure. That surely would be the worst thing that could happen, right?

But no. What Geena had actually told me to do was worse, fast worse. To have a mother in a permanent state of torture, and for there to be a wait until she was focussed again - until she was used to the pain that she was feeling inside herself and for her then to have to watch as her little girl pierced herself with a lethal looking, purpose built needle. Even when I was thinking about it back then, what I was hearing from Geena was shocking. It was more than shocking. But when I think back now, there had been a lot of sadistic thoughts put into that relatively simple instruction. Thought about the action itself, me pushing that needle through the base of each of my solid hard rubbery nipples, but then the result of that on mum. And then the thinking of the reasoning behind it. All of this just so that I would have the possibility of being put into that orgasmic state again. There was that to think of as well. The reasoning behind what I had to do. Maybe I could have just refused and seen what happened. Mum had played her part after all. Maybe I would get the orgasm after all, if I just refused.

But I couldn't. I couldn't refuse. In my mind and in my body there was just too much at stake. Too much that I might miss out on if I refused to do it now. And then there was the thought that I might be in for far worse torture if I didn't go through with something that I had promised to do. I had to do it. And there was the creek and squeak of my rubber cat suit as I adjusted myself on that seat. I was watching mum. I was watching for signs of her coming down from the intense pain she was in. Looking for signs that she had and was absorbing it. That her body was accepting it. And looking for signs of clarity in her eyes.

I needed her to know what was going on around her. I needed her to be aware of what I was doing. Geena didn't say or do anything. She just stood back and watched. I was feeling that I was so close now to being granted that pleasure again that I wanted and needed to do this right. I already knew deep down inside that I shouldn't be doing this, that I shouldn't be showing my own mother what I was about to do to myself. But I had already discounted that and was going to do it anyway.

"Mum. Mum I want you to try to focus on me for a little while. I want to show you something. I want you to see what I am going to do to myself. What I have to do myself just so that I can feel that orgasm again." I was more than aware of the dripping quality of my own voice. The sexual need had changed my voice. It had done that on a permanent basis. It was like one of the changes that Geena had inflicted on me. She had turned me into a dripping sexual freak and it was important that my voice matched. And that was what it did in this red rubber room. My voice must have snapped mum out of her own mire to an extent.

Her eyes flicked round as though they were searching for me. And at first they went to the platform that I had been on for a long time. That was the last she had been aware of me. But then they flicked to me on the chair. She was with me. I could see the clarity in her eyes. She was still dealing with the pain but it was like her mind and her body had got over the initial shock of that pain and now she was dealing with it. And now to an extent she was multi-tasking again. Something that women were good at, so the legend goes.

I shifted on the chair and sat with my ballet boots wide on the floor. My knees were wide as well. I didn't see the point in hiding my stretched, abused and dripping sexuality from my mother, not given these circumstances. And as well and that I was in the mind that I needed the orgasm back and to do that I needed to impress Geena. So, I sat wide and proud. I came to edge of the seat and I displayed myself for my mother. And the thing was that it worked. She was looking right at me. I don't know what she was thinking or even if she was thinking at all. But she was looking right at me. The pain was written all over her face but the clarity and the awareness was in her eyes.

There was a little sucking in of air as I pushed that needle through my first nipple. I sucked in air a little bit, but mum's sucking in of air was more acute, and with more volume. And her eyes were wider. Like she was shocked by what she was seeing. I understood that. But I sat up straighter, as though I was in a stage of rebelling against her or something. Me in my rubber and with my dripping sex and huge nipples. And my mum in shock by what she was seeing. I was shocked as well. Shocked by how easy that needle was to push through the base of my nipple. Yes, I was shocked by that. But that needle was designed to do what it did. It wasn't designed to make the act of piercing intimate flesh difficult. But I was shocked by how easy it was to push the needle through.

There was a little pain. Like a pain that interrupted and disturbed the deep-seated throb that existed in each nipple. But truth be known I expected it to hurt. I think I expected it to hurt more than it did. I thought it would be harder to push the needle through the solid rough flesh and I thought it would hurt more. Wrong on both counts. But because I was wrong, I was able to watch and look directly at mum as I pierced the base of each nipple. It was like I wanted her to watch, I wanted her to see what I was doing. I wanted her not to miss any part of what I was doing. I wanted her not to miss a single nuance of what was happening just a few feet in front of her. And there was that shock, pure undiluted shock written all over her face. She was having to deal with the pain and she was having to deal with the shock as well.

Geena didn't say anything she just watched. Like she was taking it all in. It was like she couldn't take enough in all at once but she was trying. Her eyes flicking from me to mum and back again. There was this smile on her face and that made me feel a little better. If she was smiling then in my fucked-up mind she was pleased and I may get the orgasm. But that was the strange thing. I wasn't taking for granted that I would be given the orgasm just because I was doing as I was told. I was kind of wondering or hoping that I had done enough for her to grant me that. As I 'fucked' each of my nipple piercings with the needle, I was looking at Geena wondering if I had indeed done enough.

Chapter 19

Geena just watched. She watched because she didn't want to miss even a split second of what was happening. Those throbs in my pierced nipples had been disturbed. They were still there. I could feel them. But there was a secondary throb that had set in inside each nipple and that was caused by the piercings that I had given myself in front of my mother. I felt kind of proud of myself. I was sitting like I felt, high and proud on that chair with my legs spread wide and my sexuality in that constant state of drip. And mum's eyes on me. Like she couldn't believe what she was seeing, but more like she was shocked to the core by what she was seeing. I got it.

What I had done was designed by Geena to shock mum. This whole night had been designed to send tremors of undiluted shock into mum's central nervous system. I look back now and I can see that. I can see it much clearer now than I could back then. I was bemused back then. I had been taken into a world that I wasn't accustomed to. I had been taken into Geena's world and I was so young that I hadn't adapted to it. Not fully. But when I think about it now, I must have been putty in Geena's hands. And mum even more so.

"Take a thicker needle out of the case Tara. Actually, take two thicker needles out of the case and push them through the holes that are already there. Make them bigger. But this time leave the needles in place. Think you can do that for me Tara? Think you can show mum what a good girl you are." I could feel my tongue running across the underside of my top lip. The hope was still alive - the need was still alive. Geena hadn't called time on my attempts, or mum's attempts to get me back into the orgasmic state so that had to be good. I was just having to do a little bit more. That was alright. I understood that. I didn't answer Geena. I just kind of nodded with my eyes and she smiled at me as I selected the thickest of the needles in that little velvet case. Then mum made a sound. Like she was pulling herself together. She sniffed and then she spoke, "Please, please Tara, don't do it baby. Let's just get out of here. This woman can't do this to us, it's wrong. Tell her no and let's get out of here."

Mum's voice wasn't very convincing. The words were good but there was no real belief or passion behind them. It was like the last line of defence inside my mother had spoken. But that last line of defence was like a last breath of a dying woman. Geena didn't say anything to mum's words at first. She just watched her, and she looked from mum to me and then back again. It was like she was interested if mum's words had had any effect on me what so ever. But this time I was holding those two thicker needles and I was ready to push them through the smaller holes that I had made earlier. And those needles I was holding now were thicker by some amount. I could feel the different thickness and weight in them. That made me shudder a little bit. And for Geena it was like she was taking stock of the bedlam and the chaos she had caused in mine and mother's lives. It was like she was just taking stock, just trying to decide if she had caused us as a mother and daughter pairing enough hurt. But I think I knew the answer to that even back then. I was more than sure that there would never be enough for Geena. She was the sort of woman who would always want more. The sort of woman who would always demand more. A true sadist maybe.

"Tina, you still have some shit to learn. Your little girl doesn't take instructions off you anymore. Did she ever? She will do what 'I' want her to do because she wants what only I can give her. She isn't going to refuse. And you both are not just going to walk out of here. You need a reality check Tina. I can understand the real world trying to drag you back in but that isn't going to happen. Now why don't you just re-adjust yourself on those dildos and watch your little girl earning her orgasms because you need to know that this will be the way that Tara has to live from now on. She will have to 'earn' the orgasmic state that she is addicted to." I don't know, it was like some sort of apocalyptic picture that Geena was painting with her words. But at the same time those words made me feel good. That I would only do what Geena told me. And that was true. That was so true because I knew that it was only with Geena that the true hope of me experiencing that orgasm was held.

I picked my left nipple first and directed the lethal point of the needle into the existing hole. There was still the rawness of the new hole so the thicker needle immediately hurt me more and I sucked in air and nibbled my bottom lip. Just at that precise time I got a whiff of the latex that I was fitted with and that was like a comfort to me. I don't know why that was, it just was. It was like I had alluded to before. The rubber skin that I was fitted with, warming me and comforting me. And that was still there and the smell and the aroma just emphasised it a little bit more. So, I pushed the needle in further until I could feel the hole being stretched and enlarged. And I kept my eyes on my mother, like I wanted her to see me doing this. I needed her to see me doing it. And Geena watched as well. But I had the feeling that she was a little bit agitated about mum's little half-hearted outburst and so she was doing something as well.

I didn't know what she was doing until mum screamed out at the top of her voice. Geena had made the things inside mum, those phallic cock like things expand and thicken a little bit more. Mum would have thought from before that they couldn't be expanded anymore. But she had been wrong. She had been told that the safety cut off devices had been removed and this was proof of that. My own nipple focussed pain as I enlarged the holes through the base of them was so so small compared to what mum was going through. For Geena, my pain was just to prove that I was doing what she told me and that I would do anything she told me.

What she was doing to mum was torturing her for daring to defy her. Or for daring to try to defy her. She was teaching her a lesson. And the lesson that she was teaching her was immediate. It was a snap torture that was acute and it was severe. The look on mum's face was something that I hadn't seen before. It was like a haunted look. She was dealing with the intense pain inside her but that look was painted on her face as much as her lipstick was painted on her lips. Like a haunted look. Like finally she knew the way it was going to be. Or finally like she didn't know where or how this thing was going to end.

Mum screamed and screamed as I pushed those needles through the original holes through my nipples. There was this pain - this intense stinging pain and that made me wince a little bit. But the further through I pushed the needles, the more I squeezed and the more I dripped to the floor under the chair I was sitting on. I wasn't even sure at this point if mum was knowing what I was doing in front of her, or if she was taking it in. She was in so much pain, causing so much din herself that it was like she couldn't possibly be taking in what I was doing because she was having to deal with her own shit. I know now that she was indeed taking it all in and that she was simply being more and more destroyed as I hurt myself in front of her like that. I know now that she was screaming with the pain but also there were silent screams coming from her because she could do nothing more to help me or protect me. I know now that it was at this precise time that she lost me. That she couldn't fulfil her role as my mother any longer and that she had simply lost me.

I try to imagine what this must have been doing to her. It was a good job that I couldn't work it all out back then because that would have been like a torture to me. For me at that time, I just had to do what Geena wanted so that she would play with that little remote-control thing again and send me into raptures of pleasure. That was all I had in my mind. That was all I needed. I had already decided back then that I didn't give a flying fuck about my mother and what she was going through. I was so selfish back then. I was so self-centred. I was so 'it's all about me'. And that was the truth. As far as I was concerned that orgasmic state was mine and I wanted it. I didn't just want a little bit of it, I wanted it all. If mum had to suffer then so be it. If I had to suffer then so be it. But I was determined to get that orgasm back. Even through the doubts that I had, the little paranoid doubts that all addicts get that I wouldn't get my next fix at all, there was still this determination there - like a rock-hard steel core.

I sat on that chair in front of mum. My latexed legs were still spread and my sex lips still hung dripping between them. My feet were still severely arched into those ballet heeled boots. And there was still that pressure on my spine caused by the way I was sitting or 'posing' on that chair. And the thick needles through the bases of my nipples were still there. Those needles added a brutal element to the scene in that red glowing room. And there was the pain associated with those piercings. And from those piercings being stretched and opened up a little bit more. Once again Geena didn't say anything. She was just watching. She was watching me and she was watching mum. Her eyes flicking back and forth. Mum was in that pain. I knew she was in that pain. I could not imagine or know what was going on inside her body. But the both of her most intimate holes were stretched. They had been stretched and opened up and the inside of her would have been pummelled and there would have been times, maybe when she wasn't screaming at the top of her voice, when mum would have felt herself being destroyed cell by cell.

Geena didn't say anything for a long time. It was like she was taking in the moment. Like she was absorbing the sight in front of her. The sight of mother and daughter under her complete and utter control. She would have known by now that mum was there. That she was as much under her control as I was. Maybe it was like a pinnacle that she had reached and she needed that time just to take it all in. Maybe it was the realisation that she had just about done what she set out to do and that was to 'ruin' a young girl, me, and then top that with the ruination of my mother. A double whammy as it were. The pinnacle of her sadism so to speak.

Mum didn't really get used to that pain again. There was a point at which she could absorb it and then live with it. That had been before her little outburst. Now though, now she couldn't live with it anymore. It was a pain inside her so constant that if she moved a muscle, even if she thought about moving a muscle, then she would get a shot of acute pain that would take a little more of her sanity away from her. A pain so awful that a few more of her brain cells would be melted as she screamed and screamed and screamed. "I know you can hear me Tina. This is what you get when you defy me. And I want you to see what you get when you're a good girl like Tara has been. I want you to witness the contrast between your absolute pain and Tara's pleasure." I was listening. Did this mean what I thought it meant? I got this feeling charging through me that I had come through the 'test' and I was going to be put back into that orgasmic state. In a way I couldn't believe what I was hearing, or what I was believing.

But at the same time, I was taking in all of Geena's words and what they meant. There was that contrast between my existence and mum's. There was a shot of something, like sorrow that went through me, that mum shouldn't be suffering like this. And that she didn't deserve to be suffering like this. And that it was all because of me. And that was a fact - that it was all because of me. But then it hit me that I was so close to the orgasm again, so close to what I needed again that I couldn't let anything else sway me, or pull me off the track that I needed to be on. I felt that I was so close to that orgasm that I could feel my sexuality reacting to that. I could feel myself come alive down there. As though my cunt was breathing and just waiting for the pleasure all over again. It was like I was alive down there. I had always been alive down there, even through the worse times, but this was different. This was my sexuality craving the orgasm and feeling that it was so close that all it had to do was squeeze and it would come.

"Say pretty please Tara. Say pretty please for your orgasm." Geena spoke and she spoke with a smile. This was the smallest thing ever that I had to do just to be given that orgasm. I didn't get the degradation of it back then. I get it now. I know now that Geena was just putting the icing on the cake of the degradation that I had been inflicted with. I'm more degraded now when I think of it. Back then it was an easy thing that I had to do. "Pretty please Geena, pretty please can I have my orgasm back. Pretty please." Back then I didn't care how many times I said pretty please. I would say it a hundred times if I had to, I didn't care. But then I didn't know how degrading I was being to myself either. But then it came. The pleasure, it came again. And there was no

183

build up, or warning that it was coming. It just came. One second it wasn't there. One second all that was there was my pulsating pussy, eager and hungry for the pleasure, but then in the blink of an eye it was back and my eyes rolled in their sockets.

I groaned, and moaned and I think I grunted because that was all I could do. I would have thanked Geena for the feeling that I was getting. But that wasn't something that I could do because the rest of my systems, the rest of my head and body was busy absorbing this beautiful pleasure that Geena had granted me. I was grateful for it. I was so grateful. More grateful than I had ever been for anything in my life. I just couldn't tell her. I just couldn't let her know. But even back then I had a feeling that she knew. I had a feeling that she knew exactly how grateful I was. She had inflicted me with this addiction and so she must have known what that meant. She must have known each and everything, each and every result of my addiction was and what it meant. There were things happening inside me that were sending me into some kind of orbit. There was the creak and the squeaks of my latex, and there was the moans and groans coming from between my red lips. Those moans and groans being accompanied by drool that just escaped my mouth.

It wasn't as though I didn't know I was drooling like that. I just didn't give a flying fuck about it. All I cared about was this fucking amazing orgasm that didn't have a start, or a middle or an end. It was just 'an orgasm'. A single thing that filled every fibre of my being. A thing that filled every fibre of me with so much intense pleasure that I cannot describe it. It was maybe at this point that I realised that I wasn't like other addicts at all.

Other addicts like drug addicts, crack addicts, even alcoholics, got that buzz from their addictions in the first place, but they never achieved, or surpassed that original buzz ever. But me. I got that intense orgasm the first-time round, the one that hooked me and got me addicted. And every single orgasm that came after that superseded the original one. Each and every orgasm that I got given took me to another greater height. My addiction was the 'best' addiction. That was what I felt as I slid round on that chair. The high and proud stance was gone as those sensations reeling through me caused me to wriggle and writhe. I was just a girl trying to get the most out of something that was so fucking beautiful that I didn't give a flying fuck about anything else.

I did look at mum during that time. I couldn't help but look at her. It did register to me that she was destroyed by what was happening and what had happened in this house and in this red glowing room. It did strike me that she wouldn't ever be the same again - how could she be? But they were fleeting thoughts. Thoughts that came and went in a flash. I was too busy to let the thoughts play on my mind. I was too busy enjoying myself - too busy immersing in my addiction not even sparing a thought that my addiction was deepening with every squeeze I gave that thing inside me. It struck me, my squeezes enhanced my pleasure and mum's squeezes around the dildos inside her simply enhanced the pain she was in. The pain she was in constantly.

Chapter 20

There had to be an end to this chapter of my life. There had to be some sort of conclusion. There had to be an end game of sorts. There had to be a transition from this night that me and mum were brought back together in that house. There had to be 'something'. That night, once I had done what I had to do, once I had earned my orgasm back I could just kick back and enjoy it. I had earned it so I could enjoy it. And I did. I did enjoy it. Truth be known I couldn't do anything but enjoy it. Couldn't do anything but absorb it. I had to do that because it could be taken off me at any time. Geena could take it away at any time and leave me in that wilderness with 'nothing'. I don't think I could have bared that. I don't think my central nervous system would be able to cope with that 'nothingness' where there was orgasm. Geena played with the orgasm a little bit. She turned up and down, and twisted it around. She made me work with it, and for it. But largely she left the orgasm intact. I liked that she was a woman of her word. When she said that I could have an orgasm, she gave me one fuck of an orgasm. She gave me my reward and made that reward beyond memorable.

She left me sitting in that chair, squirming and squelching through my own juices. And I was given 'freedom' alongside that orgasm. I could get up, walk around and I could experience the beautiful thing that was my orgasm in several ways. It was funny how standing produced a different sensation than sitting. That was the boots - making everything tight. Making everything tort. And then sitting down, crossing my rubbered legs gave a completely different sensation. If I stood, and leaned against a wall like some hooker waiting for passing trade, that gave yet another sensation. But I could absorb it all. I was in my elements. The more I had the more I wanted. I knew I was greedy but I just didn't give a flying fuck.

Yes there were times when the intensity was almost overbearing. When it was almost too much for me to comprehend but I was finding the more that I had, the more that I experienced, the more I could absorb. That was the addiction simply consuming me. I understood it. It was like I could feel that addiction taking a stronger and stronger hold over me and it wasn't as though I didn't know what was happening to me and it wasn't as though I didn't know that really I should pull myself together and get out of it. But that is a simplified view. Actually doing that. Actually breaking away from that pleasure would not be an easy thing to do. Even when I didn't have the orgasm, and was working to earn it back, I couldn't walk away from it.

Even then I needed it so badly. That was because it had already made its mark on me. It had already consumed me from the very core of my sexuality and the very core of my brain. And now even knowing that with every squeeze of that thing up inside me, with every ooze of juices that seeped from me and ran down my rubbered thighs, my dependency on the orgasmic state just grew and grew. It might not have struck me so starkly, but even then I was fucked. Well and truly fucked.

Then there was mum. When my state was just growing and deepening and becoming a part of who I was and what I was, there was what was happening to mum. I kind of knew that my future was mapped out. I kind of knew that I wouldn't be allowed to just go home and play happy families ever again. But what about mum? Geena had told her that she would get to see what she had seen and then she would be taken home and made to face her torment all on her own. But then mum had had her little outburst and all that had changed. She

187

had been shown what real pain was like. And she had had it hinted at, what it would be like to live with that pain on a long-term basis. By the time Geena stopped the torture of the inside of mum, mum was a wreck. She certainly wasn't the woman, or the 'mum' that I had known. But Geena wasn't even finished with her then.

"You're going home Tina. You're going home like I said you were in the first place. You're going to have to live with this. You're going to have to live with what you've seen here. And you are going to have to live with what you know is happening to Tara." Geena stopped talking. It was like the old Geena, like the one that I had met the first time that night. It was like she was out of her zone now and she was being normal. That is, she was being as normal as she could be given the way she lived her life. Given the way she enforced her way of life on others.

She stopped talking like she always did, so that mum could comprehend and process the words she had heard. At least at this point mum wasn't in that pain anymore. And those things had been taken from her. Those phallic things that had been inflated and extended up inside her were out of her. I think I will always remember the big huge, groaning sigh that she let out when those things were taken out of her sexuality and out of her back passage. It was like a weight had been lifted off her shoulders. And it was like that pain inside he was no more. That was because it was gone.

"I want you an addict Tina - just like your little girl." And it was as though she were making this huge announcement. It sounded alright to me. But then I was bias because I was an addict of Geena's design. I mean it could have ended all a lot worse for mum. But Geena made the announcement and then stopped again. Her pauses weren't for me, I was too busy taking all of my own orgasm. Her pauses, and the way she delivered her

188

words were for mum. Mum would have been just getting over the period of intense and prolonged pain so her mind wouldn't have been totally there, not yet. And now she was having to deal with these other words from Geena. She must have been thinking 'just let me go, please, just let me go.' I could imagine her thinking like that, with the odd 'fuck' and 'bitch' thrown in there for good measure. But I knew also that whatever the circumstances of her going back home it would be hard. She couldn't unsee what she had seen, or un-experience what she had experienced in this house on this night. And she would be alone. All alone with her thoughts.

That would still be the case because there wasn't even the passing thought, or hope that I would be going home with her. I didn't even want to go home. I wanted to be with or near Geena. It was Geena that controlled my addiction and kept me fed. I wanted and needed to be as near to her as I possibly could be. To me that was non-negotiable. I couldn't begin to imagine what mum was going to have to go through. As it happened there was some of it I wouldn't have to imagine because I would see it first-hand. "You're going to be fitted with a chastity device Tina. You will not be able to remove this. It will be locked on and permanent. And you will be fitted with a catheter to allow for your toiletting. The design of the chastity device will allow for your needs at the other end. Other than this device, you will be free to go about your life."

There was something that wasn't quite right about that in my mind. Mum being free to go about her life. It couldn't possibly be as simple as that. and of course it wasn't. The key was this chastity device. And that was churning round in my mind as the same time as my orgasm was raging through me. Mother wouldn't be able to play with herself or stroke herself. She wouldn't be able to orgasm at all because of this device. That was

189

what chastity meant! But then she would be turned into an addict as well. I already knew how clever with 'gadgets' Geena was. She had demonstrated that with me and this thing she had fitted me with. I had a feeling that what was in store for mum was something that would probably eventually tip her into a complete and utter madness. I absorbed and lapped up my never-ending orgasm but as I did that I was also concerned for mum. Very concerned.

My concern for my mother was justified it seemed. The chastity device didn't look like one at all. It was a fitted panty girdle thing that hugged her curvy hips and ass tightly. From what I could make out it was made of thick, black industrial latex and it did shape and hug mum down there. But this thing, this 'contraption' completely concealed her sexuality. It fitted and was locked between her legs. There was a little hole for the catheter to be fed through. And this hole for this purpose gave away how intricately designed and implemented it was. It was as though this thing had been made to measure for mum. The tightness, and the fit of this item was pretty scary if I am to be honest.

I had watched Geena relieve mum of her hair down there. She had waxed her legs, her butt and her sex. I had never seen mum completely hairless and smooth like that. But that was so that this thing could be as close to her skin, to be as much her skin as possible. And there was a hardness to the latex, and a moulded quality to it. There would be no feeling herself through that thing. It was just too hard, just too shell like. And yet the fit of it, the design of it would enable anything to be worn over it. It was a complete encapsulation of mum's femininity.

And then there was the hidden trickery. And there had to be some. Geena had got mum to sit with her legs spread as she had fed the catheter through the hole and down into her bladder. I had been experiencing higher

190

levels of orgasm that I had to date, but it was like I stopped in my tracks to watch when Geena was doing that. She had slipped on latex, surgical gloves and she had handled the catheter like she had done it before, a number of times. And then she just pushed it into mum. Like she knew where the end of that catheter was going and how much of it she needed to be inside mum. And as she had done that she had spoken to mum. "Your sexuality will be teased and coerced, but there will be no orgasm. You will WANT one, but there will not be one. The teasing and the coercion of your sex will be constant. Morning noon and night. You will go through phases - at first you won't be able to sleep because of what the device will be doing to you. Then you will come to live with it, to an extent. You will get some sleep, of sorts. But then the maddening, truly maddening need to orgasm will be with you for a period of time. This isn't an exact science, so a time line cannot be given."

Even I was shivering at mum's immediate future. I was having trouble imagining what it would be like for her. There I was with more orgasm than I could handle and there was mum with none. She wouldn't know about the addiction yet. That was something that she would know about as Geena was at pains to point out. "Eventually you will become an addict to something that you won't have experienced. I could try to explain or describe to you what it will be like, but I wouldn't be able to do it justice. If I say that you will be existing in a hell on earth, then that will do for now. Oh, and before I forget, this chastity is tamper proof. If you even as much as TRY to get it off, well, it will be end game in more ways than one. Let's just say that you won't survive the attempt or the aftermath of the attempt." And she stopped talking again. She especially wanted those words to sink into mum's psyche. The warning of what

191

the future held and the warning of what would happen is she tried to remove the device. Mum was coming round now and she was understanding more of what she was being told.

The look on her face though. That was what I would never forget. With what she had been through and with what she was being told about her future - all the words and all of the imagining that had conjured up was casting a shadow over her face. Mum had always been stunning - attractive - pretty and she still was. But she was different now. Now that she had an idea of the future she was different. There was no hint from Geena about the longer-term future of mum. Just that she would be turned into this addict - and that was it. Nothing about what would happen after that. I didn't even know where to begin to imagine what that longer-term future would be. Come to think of it, I didn't know anything about my long-term future either. I was so consumed with the need and the greed for this orgasm that I didn't spare it a thought. Like deep down I was just assuming that THIS would be my future.

A month later

Sitting in front of a well-lit dressing table was a woman, or a man - it wasn't clear which. It was the clown suit and the clown makeup - that downturn of the mouth and the hint of sharp pointy teeth. It was only with a genuine smile across that scary look that it became obvious it was a woman. The woman Geena. She had another kids party to attend. She had another mother to suss out. Another single mother with a daughter. Behind her, standing was another clown - another scary clown. That was the man. Rob the mute. And they both looked at each other in the mirror. Now both of them were smiling.

192

In a little cage, at the back of the same room was me. My wrists were cuffed to the bars of the cage high up, and my ankles were cuffed wide apart to the bars at floor level. My sexuality was dripping like a fucked-up tap and that orgasm was melting the last of my mind. If I was asked what day of the week it was, or what time it was, I wouldn't know. It wouldn't matter any way, it wouldn't make any difference to me what time it was or what day of the week it was. I didn't know how long I had been here and I didn't know how much longer I had here. I remembered the clown at the party, my party - then it was only the one clown. That must have been Geena. She had been the one at my party. It all made sense in my mind but it didn't matter anymore. Nothing mattered any more except the juice sapping orgasm between my legs. I am signing off now. I don't have anything else to say. Nothing I say would matter anyway.

Where I used to live

Tina was sobbing. All she was wearing was a pair of fitted knee length back boots with spiked heels. She always wore heels these days because they brought her closer to the orgasm she would never get. At least would never get in the immediate future. And she was wearing the chastity device of course. There was a vacant expression on her face. Like a tired expression. One that told that she wasn't getting much, if any sleep. And one that told if she was getting sleep of any duration and quality, it was a disturbed sleep. That thing she had been fitted with had been working on her 24/7 for a whole month. But then she wouldn't know how long it had been. She would have lost track after a few days. She was smoking and she was drinking wine. Pretty much she was housebound as the process of turning her into an

193

addict was underway. She couldn't go out because there was just too much for her to contend with. She wanted to touch herself down there and she did. but it was like her fingers gave no sensations to her sexuality through the organic but armour like latex.

She was never like that - she never wanted or needed to touch herself. But now she did. She didn't just want to touch herself but she needed to. But she couldn't. She could stroke and scratch the latex 'shell' of the device that was almost organic in its fitting. But there was no sensation that would be fed through to her sexuality from the touching like that. There was nothing, no matter how hard she tried. And that simply worked on her mind as much as the inner surface of that chastity device worked on her sexuality. She was in a battle that she couldn't win. She was in a battle that she was destined to simply lose. There was no way that she could get out of the dire that she was in. There was no 'out' for her. Every so often Geena visited. Gave her some words to feed on. Checked out her vital signs. Assessed when it would be ready to take her to the next stage. That wouldn't be yet though. So, she paced the rooms in the house alone. All alone. The memories of her old life and of her sweet daughter Tara became fewer and further between. Maybe they would be reunited at some point in the future. Maybe! But then all that would do would be to regurgitate the torture and the torment. But then, as a sadist, Geena would welcome that.

"Please, please, please god let me cum. Let me cum. Let me cum!" And it was like Tina was pleading to god, or 'a' god. She did that fairly often. It was like a way that she could de-pressurise - if there was such a thing. "There is no god Tina, just me." Except it wasn't just Geena. It was her and Rob the mute. It was time for Tina to service Ron the mute orally - something, one little thing that she could look forward to in her fucked up

194